LAURA BURTON
JESSIE CAL

BURTON & BURCHELL LTD

COPYRIGHT

The characters and storylines are fictitious, and any resemblance to real-life people and events are purely coincidental. The authors retain all of the rights to this work which may not be copied and distributed online or elsewhere without the written permission of the owners of the rights.

All rights reserved by Laura Burton and Jessie Cal 2021.
First Edition
Published by: Burton & Burchell Ltd

This book is written in U.S. English

Edited by: Susie Poole

Cover Design: Writing Avalanche

❀ Created with Vellum

CHAPTER 1

Belle

Belle entered Prince John's wedding ball disguised in a beautiful light-yellow dress. It had been a long time since she had worn a corset. The boning kept her back perfectly straight and she could hardly breathe. Nevertheless, she picked up her heavy skirts and plastered on her best smile as she walked among the dancing lords and ladies.

As much as she wanted to give her condolences to the young new bride he found to take her best friend's place, Belle held back the urge by focusing on the real reason she was there.

The Prince began to dance with his new bride in the center of the room. She had a painfully narrow waist and a mass of blonde curls sitting on the crown of her head. She looked at Prince John with sparkling eyes, dazzled by her new husband and perhaps marveling at her luck. The guests' attention was respectfully glued to the couple as they formed a circle around them. Belle headed to double doors that led to the garden, but before she could grasp the brass handle, a hand grabbed hers and swung her around.

"Fancy meeting you here," King Emmett said with what he must've thought was a charming smile. He was only a year older than her and had a finely groomed head of dark brown hair, a square jaw, and a sly smile that only few were not enchanted by. But his charm hadn't worked with her in the past, and it wasn't about to work on her now. "Where are you off to in such a hurry?"

"I'm not in a hurry," Belle retorted. Her voice was slightly higher than usual, but Emmett didn't seem to notice.

"Good." His smile grew wider. "Then you wouldn't mind doing me the honor of a dance?"

"Actually, I *do* mind." She pulled away from him. "Now, if you'll excuse me, I need some fresh air."

She turned toward the double doors again, but they flung open and in walked the sheriff. She spun around before he could recognize her. After all, he'd seen her with Red and her brother, Will, the night they were captured.

"On second thought…" She grabbed Emmett's broad hand and dragged him to the very center of the dance floor, which by that point had filled with couples dancing around The Prince and his bride. She picked a spot out of the sheriff's line of sight and allowed Emmett to lead.

"So, what are you really doing here, Belle?" Emmett asked as they swayed together. "Because it can't possibly be for John. We all know he's too much of a cad for your taste."

"No wonder you're such good friends."

He narrowed his eyes. "And yet, you're dancing with me."

She gave an innocent shrug. "I figured I

already had the invitation from your sister's wedding, so why not?"

At the mention of Marian, Emmett's expression grew serious. "Have you seen her?"

Belle nodded. "She's doing well. No thanks to you, of course."

Emmett looked away from Belle, and she wondered what it was he didn't want her to see in his eyes.

"Spare me the guilty conscience act," Belle said, capturing his attention again. "I see right through you."

"Is that right?" He flashed her another smile, then twirled her around before pulling her into his arms again. His ocean-blue eyes peered into hers. "And what do you see?"

"I see..." she whispered, holding back tears as memories of that night flooded her mind. "A killer."

He let out a dry chuckle. "Hate me all you want, but I did you a favor by killing that wolf."

Belle bit back against tears at his words. Will's brother was not a beast. "He was the most loving—"

"Until you got on his bad side," Emmett

spoke through gritted teeth. "Don't you get it? No matter how nice or kind they may seem while in their human form, those beasts are wild savages. And if you get in their way, they will maul you without hesitation."

Belle was taken aback by the degree of hatred in his tone. Though she'd heard him say those exact words years ago, moments before he pulled out his silver sword and ran outside to the garden, she had never noticed pain behind them until tonight.

"What did the wolves do to you, Emmett?"

He stopped dancing and stepped back with another charming smile. Though this time she could tell it was a mere mask to hide the truth. "Thank you for the lovely dance. Always a pleasure." He took her hand and kissed it lightly before walking away.

As she watched him leave the main hall, she couldn't ignore the nagging feeling that he was hiding something. Not that it surprised her. Emmett had never been known for his honesty. And it wasn't like she didn't have her own secrets. After all, she wasn't there for the wedding.

She looked around for the sheriff. He had settled by the banquet table, talking to a young lady who looked far too young and innocent for a man like him. But Belle couldn't be bothered with such insignificant matters at the moment. She gave one last glance around the ball, then headed out the double doors.

Winter had ended, and the spring's starry night was cool and clear, an unnatural calmness filling the air. It was a stark contrast to Belle's thumping heartbeat, drumming against her ribcage. She held her breath as she struggled not to trip on the hemline of her dress or stumble over the gravel. With every step, her body tensed. And as she left the gardens, her ears began to ring.

After hurrying into the darkened woods behind the palace, she followed the trail until she came to a willow tree. Kicking some leaves aside, she found an iron door handle on the ground. It was heavy as she yanked on it, and the door dropped open with a thud. She gave one last look around to check that she was alone, then climbed down the iron ladder to a dark underground tunnel.

She took one of the lit torches from the

wall and walked down the tunnel as the flames danced on the rocky walls around her. The anticipation grew to a fever pitch as she pressed on. After rounding two corners, she finally came to a thick iron door. Without wasting any more time, she pulled out the key she'd taken from Snow at Aria's castle and stared at it for a long moment.

It was made of Elven copper with ancient markings branded on the side. She had envisioned this moment for so long, and now that it had arrived, she took a moment to regain her composure. She sucked in a ragged breath, both excited and nervous.

Finally, she exhaled, resolved and ready to face whatever she might find. She gritted her teeth as she forced the key into the lock. *There was no going back now*, she thought as she turned the lock. She listened for the sound she knew would come. And then it clicked.

The iron door squeaked as it opened slowly. The light of the torch bathed the darkened room in a fiery glow. She stepped inside with her heart thumping in her chest. She knew who she was looking for, but she had no idea what she would find.

A groan came from the corner of the empty room coupled with the sound of heavy chains dragging against the floor. Belle swung around, pointing her torch toward the sound. The fire illuminated a pair of black boots, scuffed and worn. A thick chain snaked around one leg, and Belle raised her gaze to the black shirt, hanging like rags. Just as she reached his head, the man turned away from the light of the flame, as if it hurt his eyes, and crouched on the floor with his back to her. He groaned again, but this time like he was in agony. He curled up on top of a pile of dirty blankets, pulling the chains with him.

"I'm sorry," Belle whispered, moving the fire away from him. "I didn't mean to startle you." Her eyes followed the chains made of Elven copper, just like the key that had him imprisoned. "I'm looking for Nathaniel," she added. "Is that you?"

When the man didn't respond, she took a careful step forward. Though this time she kept the torch pointed in the other direction.

"I'm not going to hurt you," she said as she crouched next to him, her voice soft. "I'm here to release you."

CHAPTER 1

"Who are you?" the man asked, his voice strained as if he'd been screaming all day. Or perhaps all his life.

"I'm Belle," she said, craning her neck to try to get a look at him as he hid in the shadows. "Are you Nathaniel, the scientist?"

He shook his head then pulled his knees to his chest. "I don't know," he said, wrapping his arms around his legs, the chains dragging next to Belle's foot. "I don't know who I am."

Belle had never actually seen a picture of Nathaniel before. She'd only ever read about his research. The cure.

The distant sound of footsteps caught Belle's heightened hearing. She closed her eyes to focus on which direction the heavy boots were coming from and how far away they were. They didn't seem to be headed their way. Not yet.

"Okay, well..." She turned back to the prisoner. "We don't have much time. If you want to make it out of here, we have to go now."

The man turned around slowly, and Belle gasped. She had expected to see a man's face, but instead a black iron mask stared back at her. Eyes like moons shone through two holes and bore into her. Belle swallowed and resisted the urge to stagger back. "What have they done to you?" she muttered, horrified.

"I don't remember," he said, looking down at his hands. "Are you able to remove these?" He lifted his bruised wrists, showing Belle the copper chains. She couldn't help but notice lines upon lines of redness and scarring up his forearms.

"I think so," she said, composing herself. After placing the torch carefully on the ground, she turned to him and lifted the copper key that was still in her hand. "May I?"

He stretched out his arms, and she fit the key into the hole. As soon as she turned it, it clicked, and the shackles fell to the ground with a loud clang. The man lifted his hands in front of his face, his gentle eyes wide as if he couldn't believe it.

The sound of footsteps was much closer than before, and Belle sniffed the air. "Someone's coming," she said, grabbing the torch and jumping to her feet. "We must go." She offered him a hand. "Come with me."

The man stood, then stared at Belle's outstretched hand for a long moment.

"You can trust me," she assured him. "I promise."

He looked up to meet her eyes, then gave her a single nod before taking her hand.

CHAPTER 2

Nathaniel

Nathaniel's mind raced with questions. Who was this woman, and what motivation brought her to find him? How did she know where he was, and why couldn't he remember anything? His mind grew dark as he tried to think about the past. It was as if someone had blotted out all of his memories with black ink.

As the carriage rocked and his brow hit the hard casing of the iron mask, every part of his body screamed in pain. He slumped and fell in and out of fitful sleep until he decided that it was not worth his energy to dwell on questions.

Finally, the carriage stopped.

"Are you able to stand?" The woman's voice was gentle, but it had a sense of urgency to it.

Nathaniel willed his limbs to move, but as he tried, his knees shook of their own accord, and he stumbled out of the carriage. He turned, casting his eyes about the darkness. His sight fell on a cabin illuminated in silver moonlight.

"Come on, let's get you inside."

A pair of hands grasped his arm, and it took all of Nathaniel's resolve not to jump out of his skin. Something about being grabbed made him feel uneasy.

Once inside, Nathaniel staggered to a chair and sat down as the woman left the room and returned with a large pail of water. She placed it on a grate over the fire logs and set to work on lighting the fire. Nathaniel watched her for several minutes, wondering what this woman's intentions were and whether she really was to be trusted. Finally, tiny embers drew a giant breath and the fire crackled, casting a warm glow across the cabin.

Books and papers covered a small wooden table in the corner, and a bearskin hung on the wall. The cabin had a strong smell of spices, which made Nathaniel's stomach ache with hunger. He remembered food, so that was a good sign. Though he had no memory of the last time he ate.

Thick, dark lashes framed the woman's brown eyes as she appeared into view. Nathaniel stared at her, taking in her appearance. The tip of her tongue peeped out from her lips as she hummed with concentration.

"Let me get you out of this barbaric contraption," she muttered, looking down. Nathaniel took the moment to retrace his steps and remember the name she had given him.

Belle.

French. Meaning... beauty. His brain recalled that information with ease. *And it was a fitting name for her*, he thought.

Her doe eyes were big and wide, and her skin had an olive tone to it. Nathaniel imagined she tanned easily in the sun. A sweep of brown hair covered her forehead and a mass of curls fell to her shoulders.

A little line formed between her brows, then a click prompted her to smile. "Here we go," she said, triumphant.

Nathaniel winced as the heavy mask squealed open and she removed it from his head.

"There, that feels better, right?" Belle said, turning away and setting the mask down on a nearby table.

Nathaniel stretched his neck and twisted his head from left to right, relieved to be free. Belle turned back with a smile which promptly dropped at the sight of him.

"Oh my…" she whispered, her hand flying to cover her open mouth.

Nathaniel wondered just how ugly he must look for Belle's face to twist in horror. Was he deformed? Perhaps that was the reason he had the iron mask on in the first place.

"You look just like…"

"An ogre?" Nathaniel finished for her. But the word made her pause.

"No," she said, brushing strands of hair away from his forehead.

The graze of her fingertips left a burning trail across his skin, but Nathaniel couldn't decide if it was a painful sensation or a longing to connect with another person.

"You look like the image of..." She dropped her hand and looked down with her brows furrowed. "It's impossible. Marian never mentioned..."

"Marian?" Nathaniel echoed. The name lit up a glimmer of recognition, but the memories were just out of reach.

Belle met his gaze, hopeful. "You know Marian?"

Nathaniel shook his head. "Who do I look like?" he asked, bringing her back on topic. If he didn't look like an ogre, perhaps he looked like a person. Perhaps this mystery woman might be the key to finding out who he was, and why he had been locked up in chains.

"You look like... King Emmett."

Nathaniel shook his head, still having no idea who Belle was referring to.

"Wait, I have a drawing of him somewhere," Belle said. She got up and hurried to the table, looking through stacks of papers. "Here." Upon her return, she thrust a piece of parchment in Nathaniel's hands. He looked down to see a drawing of a man with dark hair, deep-set eyes, and a confident stance.

"I look like him?" Nathaniel asked, looking up at Belle again. The man in the paper had broad shoulders, a squared jaw, and looked nothing like Nathaniel imagined himself to be. Belle tilted her head to the side as she studied him.

"You need to clean up and have a good meal." She got up, grabbed the pail of water with a bundle of her skirts, and bid him to follow.

They walked into a small kitchen with dead rabbits hanging from the ceiling. Belle walked past, then shouldered the back door open and marched out.

"Come on," she called back to him.

Nathaniel's head throbbed as his mind spun once more. "Why do I look like that Emmett person?" he asked, following Belle. The night was cool as they walked across the backyard. A tin bath was shielded by waist-height wood fencing. Nathaniel watched Belle stoop down, pouring hot water into the half-filled tub.

"It won't be very warm, but that should take the edge of it," Belle said, dusting off her hands and turning back to him. "I'll get you a change of clothes and a towel."

As she went to leave, Nathaniel touched her arm. "Why are you doing this for me? How did you find me?"

Belle's eyes stretched wide as they flickered down to look at his hand on her arm. He let go, stunned by her reaction.

She smiled at him. "I'll prepare some food. Don't worry, I'll tell you everything soon."

Nathaniel nodded, though he was not satisfied. He wanted answers, but he supposed he could wait a short while longer to find them.

After Belle returned with some clothes, Nathaniel made sure the door clicked shut when she left before he got undressed. He pulled the ties on his shirt undone and lifted the thin material over his head. He moved stiffly as his muscles protested. Bones stuck out and bruises covered his body. Nathaniel looked down at himself. He was malnourished. A silver ring sat on his right index finger. He took it and dragged it across his forearm. Even in the dim moonlight, the dark line was unmistakable. He was definitely anemic.

But how did he know that? Was he a doctor?

He slipped into the bathwater and inhaled deeply. Belle was right, the water was tepid at best, but the resistance of the water lifted the weight of his body, giving his bones a much-needed rest.

He was just beginning to relax when a howl in the woods caused him to bolt upright. His heartbeat thumped against his eardrums, sounding like an army of soldiers on the approach. Belle had taken him from a cell. He was locked up. Surely that meant someone was looking for him?

He took a bar of soap and scrubbed his entire body as well as his beard, hoping that the lavender scent might wash away his dark thoughts too.

Upon his return to the kitchen, he picked up the smell of meat sizzling on the stove. His stomach grumbled again, and he licked his dry lips. Belle had changed into a simple beige dress with a white apron tied at the waist. She scooped her hair into a knot at the back of her neck and a twist of curls hung to her narrow waist. Nathaniel's stomach growled again, this time louder, and must have announced his arrival because Belle glanced over her shoulder. Upon seeing him cleaned up, she did a double-take, then turned to face him.

"Now there's no mistaking it," she said, her eyes looking him up and down. "You really do look like him."

Nathaniel became uneasy. She eyed him as if she could see all of him. With nothing hidden. Then her gaze settled on his and her face softened.

"Please, take a seat."

Nathaniel dragged a chair away from the little table in the kitchen and sat. Belle handed him a cup of water and he drank. As soon as the cool liquid touched his lips, he gulped it down without barely breathing. It felt like it had been days since his last drink. Once he was done, Belle placed a plate of seared meat in front of him. He wasn't sure what kind, but as he bit into it, the strong juices told him it was game meat. Venison, perhaps.

Belle sat at the table across from him, laced her hands together, and stared at him as he ate. If Nathaniel hadn't been so hungry, he might have been bothered, but he supposed she was waiting for him to finish eating before she answered his questions.

Finally, he finished, dabbed his mouth with a napkin, and sighed. "Thank you."

Already he could feel his strength returning, and Belle's eyes twinkled at him. But then her smile faded, and she leaned forward.

"You're Nathaniel. Emmett's twin brother," she said, her voice low. Nathaniel blinked as the words registered.

"And Emmett is…?"

Belle sat back and huffed. "Arrogant. Selfish. The biggest fool in the kingdom," she began. Then, as if realizing her words, she sat up again and blushed. "I mean, he's the King of White Rose Kingdom. As far as I know, you were the rightful heir to the throne after your parents died, but before your coronation, Emmett announced that you had died at sea. Marian never confirmed it, but she also never denied it. And considering where I found you, it seems that…" She looked away in thought. "Emmett must've sold you to Prince John to take your throne."

Nathaniel shook his head. "Sorry, I'm not following." He didn't recognize any of those names. Except Marian. Though he could not put a face to the name. "I'm a king?"

"You were supposed to have succeeded your father," Belle explained. "But you never had your coronation. You've been presumed dead for five years."

"Is that why you came for me?" he asked.

Belle sighed. "No. I came for you because I was told Prince John was keeping *the chemist* in his dungeon. I've read your papers from six years ago. They were published in the books I've been researching, but you never used your real name. You only ever described yourself as *the chemist*, so I didn't know your true identity."

"What sort of papers did I publish?"

"You've written more articles on blood than anyone," she explained. "And before your disappearance, you were on the brink of discovering a cure."

"A cure for what?" Nathaniel asked, wondering what wretched virus might be ravaging the kingdom. Cholera, dysentery... more words began to cross his mind. How did he even remember those things, yet nothing about himself?

Belle lifted the sleeve of her dress and edged closer to him. "This," she said heavily. Her sweet breath tickled Nathaniel's cheek as she leaned in and held out her arm to show a curved scar. Nathaniel traced over it with his finger.

"A wolf bite," he noted.

Belle studied his eyes before she nodded, then she sat down.

He wasn't sure if it was the revelation or the absence of her body heat that gave Nathaniel a chill. "You're a wolf?"

Belle looked away. "I have read every medical journal, visited healers, listened to the whispers in the villages... searching for a cure."

Nathaniel kept silent, sensing she wasn't finished. She bit her lip and tucked a strand of hair behind her ear, tormented by her own thoughts.

"When I found your work, I finally had hope. But you were gone. Nothing has been printed with your name for years. I feared that you might have died. But then I heard about a chemist being held in his dungeon.

That was when I knew Prince John was up to something. There are rumors that his brother, King Richard, is not well. I worried that he had you slowly poisoning the King, so he could take over the throne."

Nathaniel swallowed nervously. Had he been truly embroiled in such a plot? The thought sent his stomach churning. "But you think I'm the brother of the King? Does that mean I'm Prince John's uncle?"

Belle snapped out of her thoughts and laughed. "What? No. Emmett is from another kingdom. Prince John had you locked up in Sherwood. *His* kingdom."

"And Prince John was using me to poison his brother?"

Belle shrugged. "We don't know that for sure, I'm just trying to connect the dots. What I do know is that Emmett must have sold you to Prince John. They're not just friends, but allies, you see."

"Why would my own brother sell me?" Nathaniel asked.

Belle's expression turned sympathetic. "To be king. He must have done it to get you out of the way so he could take the throne. But why Marian never mentioned you…"

"Marian is my sister?" Nathaniel asked, starting to put things together.

Belle nodded. "And she's a close friend of mine. Don't worry, she's safe."

Nathaniel slowly nodded, his head growing heavy. It was like the weight of the iron mask was back on his shoulders. He could only imagine the lengths she had gone to in order to break him out of his cell. All because she thought he could find a cure for her.

"I don't have any memories. None at all," he confessed. Belle reached out and placed her hand on his arm.

"Then we need to help you get them back," she said softly. Her touch sent a warm glow over Nathaniel's body, and for a moment, the sensation eased his troubles. But then she squeezed before letting go, making Nathaniel feel cold again.

"In the meantime, I think it's best that we keep you hidden. Prince John will have his guards looking for you, and if any of Emmett's men saw you, the recognition would be immediate, and they may have you killed."

Nathaniel shook his head. "But I don't want his throne."

Belle gave him a gentle look. "And I wish that was enough."

Nathaniel nodded. "Right. Well, any ideas on how to bring back someone's lost memories?"

A grin spread across Belle's face. "I know just the people to talk to."

CHAPTER 3

Belle

Belle jolted from bed to a dark room with echoes of screams inside her mind. Except they weren't inside her mind. They were coming from a village nearby. By the sound of their terror, and at this late at night, there could only be one reason.

The beast was back.

Propelled by instincts, Belle jumped to her feet and was out the window in the blink of an eye. She ran through the rain and into the woods as fast as her human legs could manage —until she shifted. Once in wolf form, the screams from miles away rose in volume like they were but a mere stone's throw away. The terror in their voices made her run faster as she weaved through the wet woods with only the light of the moon lighting her path. She pushed her legs harder, hoping this time she would arrive in time to keep him from killing any more people. She sniffed the air, trying to sense the iron smell of blood, but there was none. Not yet. The smell of damp wood was strong in the air, but it wasn't distracting enough to keep her from finding the beast's scent.

When she finally arrived at the village, the screams increased and pierced her eardrums. She hid behind a tree so as not to scare the villagers even further with two predators lurking in their midst.

She peeked from behind the tree. The village was in chaos. Not only were people running through the square soaking wet, but some were running out of their own homes. Why were they running *out* of their homes?

Then Belle saw the beast. He jumped out

of a window with a bag hanging in his mouth. She locked her crystal-clear vision on him. Though he looked like a wolf, he was different. He was the size of a bear but with the muscles of a gorilla. Not even her brother Will, as the alpha of his pack, was as massive as that beast.

She crouched to the ground, waiting to see which direction he would run to. But he didn't run. Instead, he sniffed the air, then turned his bright crimson eyes toward the woods. His breath came out in hot, thick puffs, creating a haze in the cool air in front of his face. He looked around, not fazed at all by the screams around him or scared of the crowd of men that marched toward him with weapons and burned-out torches in their hands. He slowly scanned the darkness. His beastly eyes narrowed in her direction, and a low growl ripped through his throat, slow and steady.

A challenge.

She didn't need to get a clear view of his mouth to sense the wicked grin creeping on his lips. He took off running in the opposite direction of where she was hiding, and she followed without a second thought. She hadn't planned to expose herself to the villagers, but she couldn't let him get away. Not again. If the fastest way to get to him was through the village—through the crowd of men with weapons—then it was a risk she was willing to take.

She braced herself for impact as swords scraped her skin, but in less than a second her path was free again. Usually, villagers—with their limited weapons and knowledge—were not difficult to outmaneuver. Wolf hunters, on the other hand, were almost impossible to escape. Not only did they know the right weapons to use, but they were also smart about where and when to strike to incapacitate a wolf. She was lucky there were no hunters around, but they would certainly appear by morning. Of that, she was sure.

Belle caught a whiff of the beast's scent in the air and pushed her legs harder. She couldn't see him through the darkness, but she could hear his heavy breathing ahead of her.

Stop. She demanded with her mind, but there was no response. She narrowed her eyes, trying to get inside his head. *Who are you?*

He growled in frustration and pushed

himself to run faster. Belle wondered if the reason for his sudden frustration meant that she was close to breaking through his mental barriers. She tried again, though her throbbing muscles made it hard for her to focus. But as she ran faster, her mind sharpened with just as much force.

Get out of my head!

The voice entered Belle's mind with such intensity, a jolt of alarm shot through her body. Her paw hit an overgrown root that stuck out from the ground, and she stumbled forward. Her face scraped through the dirt until a tree impacted her side, bringing her wolf body to a halt.

Belle pushed herself to her feet, her legs shaking with exhaustion. But that wasn't why she couldn't bring herself to run any further. She shook off the pain at her side, not even caring that it would most likely leave a bruise. She was too focused on trying to listen for the beast's voice again. But there was nothing. Not even the beast's steps or his ragged breathing.

Belle stood panting, staring into the darkness. The voice she heard sounded familiar, but she couldn't figure out where she had heard it before. It was that of a man, but it sounded muffled like he was underwater.

The thought of resuming the chase crossed her mind, but there was no way she would catch up to him again. He was too fast. Too agile. She hated admitting defeat, but having heard his voice was a victory in itself. She shook off the rainwater from her fur. Now, all she needed to do was figure out who it belonged to.

On arriving home, Belle dried herself and got dressed but couldn't bring herself to go back to bed. She was just about to make some tea when she heard the loud thud of something crashing against wood coming from Nathaniel's room. Picking up the lantern, she went to check on him. She pushed the door open, not even bothering to knock.

The window shutters were ajar. They had been blown by the wind and were slamming against the side of the house. Nathaniel was tossing and turning in bed as if he was having a nightmare. Belle walked across the room and pulled the window closed, locking it with the iron hook.

She turned to Nathaniel, trying to keep the lantern low so as not to shine the light on his face, but when he tossed the covers off his bare chest, she noticed the sheets were wet and he was drenched in sweat. Belle reached for a small towel inside one of the drawers, then went to sit on the edge of the bed next to him. After placing the lantern on the side table, she touched his clammy forehead. He was burning up with fever.

As she padded the towel lightly against his burning skin, he murmured something under his breath. Belle couldn't quite make out what he was saying, so she leaned in. His voice came out in a jumble of words and Belle leaned in even closer. His eyes suddenly shot open and locked with Belle's. She pulled back as he jolted upwards.

"No!" he barked, jerking back until he hit the wall behind him. "Don't touch me!"

Belle jumped to her feet and lifted her hands. "I'm sorry. I didn't mean to startle you."

"Who are you?" His voice was incoherent

while his eyes scanned the room like it was the first time he was seeing the place. "Where am I?"

"It's me... Belle."

"No." He stretched out his hands to keep her from coming any closer. He was panting and sweating, and his arms kept dropping as if he was too weak to keep them up. "Stay back."

Belle narrowed her eyes. "Nathaniel, do you not remember me?"

He dropped his head in his hands, grabbed his hair, and rocked himself back and forth. Sweat slid down his chiseled arms. "Why do you keep calling me Nathaniel?"

Belle returned to the edge of the bed with the towel in her hand. "You *are* Nathaniel... remember?"

He shook his head, confused. "No. I'm not. I'm just a prisoner."

Belle touched his arms, but he pulled away, shooting her a glare. "Get your hands off me!"

Belle pulled back, unsure of what else to do. Then he ripped out another frustrated grunt and grabbed his head again as if it were about to explode. He began murmuring under his breath once more, but Belle could only make out random words. *Darkness... shackles... chains.*

Belle frowned when she realized what was happening. He was reliving a memory. "Nathaniel, listen to me," she spoke softly. "I am not going to hurt you."

"Marian?" He looked up at Belle, but when his eyes met hers, there was an emptiness inside. It was like he wasn't there. "Is that you?"

"Yes…" Belle lied, reaching to touch his arms again. "It's me. Now, let me help you."

Nathaniel didn't push her away. "What's happening to me?"

"You're delirious because your fever is very high," she explained. "Now, I need you to lay down for me. Can you do that?"

He nodded, allowing her to position him horizontally on the bed. Belle frowned as she tucked him back in. "That's it."

She grabbed the dry cloth again, then dabbed his forehead. He shivered, clutching to the covers as his eyes rolled back. Belle wiped the sweat from his face with the cloth, then watched him for a long moment. Her heart ached for him. For his pain. For his memories.

"Emmett," he whispered like he was dreaming. "Don't do this." Nathaniel grabbed Belle's arm but didn't open his eyes. "You don't have to do this."

Belle frowned as she brushed a wet strand of hair from his face. "You will get through this," she whispered to him, her voice soft and gentle in the night. "I know you will."

Nathaniel's grip on her arm softened as she continued to shush him while wiping his forehead. When he finally quieted down, she watched him in the dim light of the candle that was still burning on the side table.

"What on earth did they do to you?"

CHAPTER 4

Nathaniel

$\mathcal{N}$athaniel awoke with a start to the sound of pots clanging in the kitchen. The smell of salty pork flooded his nostrils, making his stomach grumble. He yawned, rubbing his eyes. A weak stream of morning light peeked through the cracks in the shutters, while outside birds chirped. Nathaniel couldn't remember the last time he had heard birds singing.

He swung his legs out of the small bed and dressed slowly, wincing as his tight muscles throbbed. He trudged out of the little room and walked toward the kitchen. He stopped just outside the door, hearing a melodic singing on the other side. The corners of his mouth picked up as he listened.

Belle's voice was the prettiest sound he had ever heard. Not surprising, considering he didn't have much to compare it to. But Nathaniel's heart squeezed as he closed his eyes, letting the rich tones soothe him.

"Once upon a time, in a hallowed forest glade... a fair maiden plucked three flowers for her crown of scented may—" Something sparked within Nathaniel. Like a tiny ember flickering in the darkness. He had heard that song before, he was sure of it.

He shifted his weight from one foot to another and the floorboard creaked beneath him. The singing promptly stopped, and the kitchen door flew open. Nathaniel grinned sheepishly as he stood face-to-face with Belle. Wisps of flyaway hairs rested on her clammy cheeks as she shot him a quizzical look.

"Sorry," Nathaniel blurted out. "I was so taken by your singing just now, I didn't want to disturb you."

Belle's face softened, and she brushed her forehead with the back of her hand. "You remember me?" she asked, sounding surprised.

Nathaniel frowned. "Why wouldn't I?" he asked with a light chuckle. "We were introduced yesterday. You're Belle." Then he pointed at himself. "I'm Nathaniel."

Relief washed over Belle's face, and she bid him to follow her into the kitchen. Two steaming plates of food sat on the table, and Nathaniel licked his dry lips. Even though he had eaten last night, he could devour a whole banquet without breaking a sweat.

They sat at the table and Nathaniel took no time to tuck in. Meanwhile, Belle sat motionless, watching him. It wasn't until he had finished the last of the pork and downed his drink that he finally met her curious gaze.

"Is everything all right?" he asked, sensing that something was off. He glanced at her untouched plate of food, then at the crease between her dark brows. Even as she frowned, she was pleasing to the eyes. Her dark eyes were so intense, a single look in his direction made him nervous.

He snapped out of his daze at the realization that her full, rosy lips were moving. "...You gave me a fright last night. I've been worried about you."

"What happened?" Nathaniel asked, matching her frown.

Belle cocked her head to the side, studying him. "You don't remember waking up in the middle of the night?"

"What?" Nathaniel's pork churned in his stomach. "I slept right through until morning." Then he looked at Belle shrewdly as she bit her lip. "Didn't I?"

Belle frowned. "You were burning with fever, and you didn't recognize me."

Nathaniel shook his head. He didn't like the idea of waking up in the night and having no recollection of it. "What happened? Did I do something to you?"

"No," she assured him. "You went back to sleep. How are you feeling now?"

Nathaniel touched his own forehead. The fever was gone. "I feel fine."

"Do you have any idea how long you've been having blackouts?" she asked.

He lowered his eyes, embarrassed, then

CHAPTER 4

shook his head. "I don't recall ever having blackouts. I'm sorry I kept you up at night. I don't have to stay—"

"You don't have to go," she said, offering a kind smile. "In fact, I insist that you stay. It's not safe for you out there. One look at your face…"

"And it's immediate recognition, I know." He nodded, stroking his beard. "I guess there's no hiding with this face, huh?" He glanced thoughtfully out the window. "May I ask you a favor?"

"Sure."

He turned to meet her eyes again. "Would you tell me if things become… too much for you?"

She nodded, then smiled. "Nathaniel, rest assured, you are not the reason why I didn't get any sleep last night. I've been on edge lately, trying to protect the villages from the beast and—"

"The beast?" Nathaniel asked, picking up his cup. "What beast?"

"There's a wolf out there. Only, he's the size of a bear. They call him 'the beast' because he devours anyone who gets in his way."

"I see," Nathaniel said with a hum. They fell into silence as Belle seemed to be unwilling to talk about the beast anymore.

Nathaniel patted his thighs, thinking of something to say to lighten Belle's mood. "Tell me, what was that song you were singing?"

"Hm?" Belle finally looked at him again, her face softening once more. "Oh, it's a lullaby my father used to sing to me." Her eyes glazed over as a faint smile crossed her lips. "My father used to say it was a prophecy, but I just like the tune."

"A prophecy? About what?" Nathaniel asked, his curiosity piqued.

Belle sighed, her shoulders sagging as she traced along the wood grain on the table. "The girl plucks three flowers; a scarlet rose, a white daisy, and a golden daffodil. The scarlet rose is stuck with its own thorn. The white daisy loses its petals. And the golden daffodil shines brighter than the noonday sun."

Nathaniel rubbed his bearded chin, the bristles scratching his fingers.

"I'm guessing they're symbols..." he

began, trying to make sense of the cryptic song.

But Belle sniffed again and held up her hand, then her eyes stretched wide.

"Someone's coming," she said, rising to her feet and pushing the back chair across the cabin floor with a screech. She looked at Nathaniel with fierceness. "Go hide, now."

Nathaniel shakily got to his feet and looked around the little kitchen for somewhere to hide. The walls were crammed with shelves of jars and spices. "What are you going to do?" he asked, trying and failing to find anywhere to go.

Belle rushed him out of the kitchen and into the other room. "In here, quick." She pulled open a cupboard and nudged Nathaniel in the back. He stumbled forward and she slammed the door behind him.

"Hey, what are—" Nathaniel spluttered, turning around, but he stopped when Belle shushed him. Nathaniel peeped through the crack in the cupboard door and watched her straighten her back and hold still as if trying to listen.

Then, she gasped and bolted out the front

door. Nathaniel strained to listen out for the sound of horses or carriage wheels bumping along the stony path to the cabin. But all he could hear was a shriek that sent his heart thumping so fast, he flew out of the cupboard and ran for the window.

What he saw next had him frozen on the spot, his arms hanging limply at his sides like spaghetti noodles.

A young woman with a long red cape approached the cabin, sitting on a large brown wolf. Her hair sat in a braid over her left shoulder, and she grinned at Belle.

At least, Nathaniel thought it was Belle. The moment he blinked, her human form had vanished, and another wolf stood in its place. This one had golden fur. Nathaniel's heart jumped to his mouth as he watched the young woman jump off the brown wolf and step away. She took a few more steps to the side, leaving the two wolves to greet each other.

They played like a pair of puppies, rolling in the dirt and pawing at each other with gleeful yelps. Nathaniel didn't know who these people were, but whoever they were, Belle was comfortable enough to shift in front of them.

Overcome with curiosity, he made for the door and thrust it open to get a better look. The sound of the squeaky hinges interrupted the wolves and the brown one looked up at him. A pair of amber eyes landed on him, and Nathaniel stared back, jolted by a sudden flash of memory...

A wolf lay panting with its tongue flopped out on a dark wood table. Nathaniel picked up a needle then filled a vial with a purple liquid, but before he could administer the solution, the wolf's eyes caught his attention. He paused, and for a moment, the two of them were still. Then the wolf's pupils dilated, and the light faded from them. Nathaniel fell to his knees, sending a tray of medical instruments clattering to the floor.

Nathaniel blinked several times, his ears ringing and heart thumping so fast, it threatened to jump out of his chest. Somehow, he ended up on the floor. He squinted into the sunlight as he looked up. The two wolves had disappeared. The young woman in the red cloak dashed forward and helped him to his feet.

"Let's get you on the chair, come on," she muttered, straining under his weight.

"Where is Belle?" he asked, staggering to the wooden armchair and collapsing in it, his temples pulsing.

"They raced into the woods. She should be back in a minute. Let me fetch you some water," the young woman said, heading toward the kitchen.

Nathaniel took the moment to hold his head in his hands. He wondered if he was now suffering from hallucinations, but what he saw felt so real. It was more like a memory.

Before he could brood on it more, two voices caught his attention. It sounded like they were standing just outside the window.

"I thought we could spend some time here with you, Belle."

"You know you're always welcome, Will. It's just... I've got my hands full at the moment."

"I'm worried about Red. She's been under a lot of stress, and I'm afraid she'll get too overwhelmed with all the extra responsibility since Robin's still gone."

The sound of footsteps and a cough prompted Nathaniel to lift his head and meet the worried gaze of the young woman in the red cloak. She returned with a cup of water and a plate of crusty bread.

"I can go out and forage for some berries if you like?" she said.

Nathaniel forced a smile against his throbbing headache and took the cup and plate. "Thank you."

The front door swung open, and Belle marched in, looking at Nathaniel like he might blow up at any moment. "What happened?"

Nathaniel chewed on his lip, looking furtively from the young woman, who he presumed to have been Red, and the male, he figured must have been Will. He didn't know these people or how much he should say with them within earshot.

Belle seemed to follow his thoughts. "It's all right. This is my brother, Will, and his wife, Red. You can trust them." She shifted in her seat before she motioned to Nathaniel like a tour guide pointing out something of interest. "This is Nathaniel. Emmett and Marian's brother."

Red's eyes stretched wide but she didn't speak. Nathaniel presumed that although she must've known about Emmett, she didn't know what he looked like. Otherwise, she would have noticed it before. Will, on the other hand, kept his face perfectly neutral as he gave Nathaniel a small wave, though Nathaniel supposed this was his poker face. Nonetheless, if Belle trusted them, he supposed he could too.

Nathaniel gulped down his drink, confident he wasn't being poisoned. Then he wiped his mouth with the back of his hand and sighed as everyone sat down, staring at him.

"I think I had a flashback," he began, trying to keep his voice steady, but his insides were shaking at the thought of it. Will looked at Belle quizzically.

"He's lost his memory," she muttered to her brother, then turned back to Nathaniel. "Go on."

Nathaniel rested his forearms over his legs and exhaled with his eyes closed. He then recounted everything he could remember from the flashback. The laboratory, the vials of blood, and the syringe in his hand. When he told them about the dying wolf, he opened his eyes, catching Will and Belle exchanging a worried look.

CHAPTER 4

"So... are you some kind of wolf doctor?" Red asked.

More like a mad scientist, it seemed. Nathaniel remembered the strange-looking objects all around the laboratory. What kind of person treated wolves, anyway? From what Belle had told him, humans feared wolves.

"Not a wolf doctor," Belle said, getting up and striding over to the table littered with papers. "A chemist, with a keen interest in studying wolves." She bundled the papers and pieces of parchment in her arms and carried them to Nathaniel.

"This is everything I could get my hands on," she said. "All your published articles, annotations, and studies."

Nathaniel put down his drink on a side table and took the papers, resting them on his lap. He looked down to find writings with his name on them and scribbles along the edges that he supposed were Belle's.

"You were studying wolf DNA," Belle explained. "Trying to decipher it and find out if the gene sequence could be manipulated..."

"...to reverse the transitional process."

Nathaniel finished, though he had no idea where the thought came from.

Belle's face lit up and she gave him a smile more beautiful than the rising sun. He couldn't help but smile back.

"You remember?" she asked excitedly.

But Nathaniel's smile faded as he thought about it. He shook his head. "No. But all of this does sound familiar. My knowledge of science is still there. Everything else is just darkness."

Belle's smile faltered a little, but she fixed it to one that didn't quite reach her eyes.

"Well, it's a start."

Will cleared his throat. "Sorry to sound rude, but how did that happen? Losing your memories, I mean," he asked, looking at Nathaniel with a brow arched.

Belle huffed as she paced the room, then she spoke at rapid speed and filled Will and Red in on what happened.

"Wait," Red said, jumping to her feet with a gasp. "The key you needed us to get? *That* key?"

Belle nodded. "Prince John was keeping him in a dungeon."

Red followed Belle around the room, also in thought. "But why would Prince John want to keep him as a prisoner? And it can't just be to keep him out of Emmett's way."

"Nathaniel is a chemist," Will said, rubbing his chin. "That would make sense if the rumors are true."

Much to Nathaniel's relief, Belle and Red stopped walking to look at Will. He was getting dizzy watching them dart around. "What rumors?" Red asked.

"King Richard being sick," Belle replied. "He has been getting sicker for some time now, and there are whispers that he's under pressure to hand over the crown to his brother."

Red gasped again. "You don't think he was using Nathaniel to... to…"

"Poison the King," Will cut in. "It's possible."

Nathaniel's stomach lurched. He didn't want it to be true, but the clues seemed to point to the theory that he had in fact been poisoning the King. Whether it was or wasn't against his will... the idea that he might have been involved made him nauseous.

Belle nodded along, her brown eyes boring deep into his soul, as if she could hear his thoughts. "We don't know anything for certain. All we have is speculation," she said with a note of finality. "But it still doesn't make sense why you would've lost your memories. Unless..." She crossed the room once more, then turned back to Nathaniel. "Roll up your sleeves."

"What?" Nathaniel said, his heart racing at the urgency in her voice.

She didn't ask again, instead she marched over to him. "Your sleeves. Let me see your arms."

Nathaniel pulled up his left sleeve, revealing deep bruises. Belle dipped down and traced a finger over his skin.

"You're covered in punctures," she said. "Look here, and here... and here."

Nathaniel looked down and squinted. Belle was right. From a distance, the puncture holes might just have looked like large pores, but on closer inspection, there was no mistaking them. He looked up and met Belle's intense stare.

"You don't think they poisoned me too, do you?"

Belle dragged a hand over her face with a sigh. "There's only one way to find out."

She hurried out of the room, leaving a shocked Nathaniel looking at Red and Will, neither of whom appeared to know what to say. After a few awkward minutes of silence, and just as Nathaniel was wondering where on earth Belle had gone, Will shrugged. "Don't worry, she'll be back. When she gets an idea, she doesn't always share with the rest of us until she's processed it," he said, shooting Red a look. The corners of her mouth lifted in response.

A jingle of glass bottles announced Belle's return. She ambled into the room carrying a tray of medical equipment. Nathaniel surveyed the instruments as she knelt beside him. Cotton, a glass vial, and rubber tube.

"Are you going to draw my blood?" he asked as she picked up a brown bottle of strong-smelling liquid and stoppered it with a cotton ball.

She turned it upside down, then she gave Nathaniel a firm look. "The way I see it, the only way we can get the answers to your questions is by testing your blood."

"And you know how to do that?" Nathaniel asked.

Will snorted, which did not give Nathaniel any confidence that Belle knew what she was doing.

Belle huffed, ignoring Will. "I can draw blood. I've done it to myself many times," she explained, dabbing inside Nathaniel's arm with the soaked cotton. "But I don't have the knowledge... nor the equipment to *test* it."

Nathaniel looked around. "So, what is the plan here?" he asked. He wasn't sure he'd be able to remember how to analyze a blood sample in his current state.

"I know one person who can," Belle said, her eyes glinting.

"Who?" Nathaniel asked just as Will and Red made identical sounds of surprise. Belle placed the needle tip to his skin, then glanced at him, waiting for an approval. He gave her a single nod, and she pushed it through.

"Your sister, Marian," she said simply. "She's a healer."

Nathaniel hissed at the sharp scratch.

"My sister?" he repeated. He tried not to watch the blood dripping into the vial, realizing that he might have been a chemist, but the sight of his own blood made him queasy.

"Yes." Belle glanced over her shoulder. "I'm guessing she's in Sherwood with Robin, right?"

Red and Will exchanged looks again, both of them with wide eyes.

"Robin is missing," Red said.

Nathaniel noticed a flicker of shock in Belle's eyes, but he was grateful that she kept composed until she removed the needle. She then pressed another cotton ball on his arm.

"What do you mean, *missing*?" she asked in a measured tone.

"He was taken," Will replied. Nathaniel listened to them talk at fast speed, his mind spinning again, barely able to take in everything they were saying. Belle listened with her finger pressing harder and harder on the cotton ball as Red and Will took turns to tell her about a note left behind with a cryptic message.

"And it says only true love's kiss will bring

him back," Red said before stopping to take a breath.

"What does that even mean?" Belle asked.

"We don't know," Red replied. "We haven't even found him yet. And seeing as Marian doesn't love him, even if we find him, we won't be able to save him."

Belle let out a low whistle, then her eyes darted to Nathaniel's reddened arm, suddenly aware that she had been holding it for so long. "Sorry." After loosening the pressure, she looked at Will. "Do you know where we can find Marian?"

"She's still in Sherwood," Red said.

Belle exhaled, then held up the vial of blood to her eyes and swirled it around. "Then I'll leave it up to you to decide if you want to come or not," she said, putting the vial down again and meeting Nathaniel's stare. "Would you like to see your sister?"

He swallowed. It wasn't that he didn't want to meet his sister, but the thought of going on a long trip only to find out that she was also in agreement with Emmett in selling him off to Prince John filled him with dread. He didn't know that for sure, but he couldn't risk getting caught and being thrown back in that dungeon. Even if she didn't turn against him, meeting yet another person he had no memories of made him uneasy. He glanced at the papers on his lap.

"Maybe I should stay and look through all this," he said, trying to sound sensible. "Who knows, maybe if I read my research, it'll trigger some more memories."

Belle nodded. "Right. I'll make preparations to leave immediately." Her eyes flit from Nathaniel to Will. "You two are welcome to stay…" She raised her brows as if having a silent conversation, and Will nodded.

"It's settled then. These two will stay here and help you stay warm and fed while you focus on your research," Belle said, rising to her feet. "And I'll go and get this tested. I should be back in a couple of days." She held the vial of blood in the air like she was about to give a toast. "Here's to answers."

CHAPTER 5

Belle

Belle heard Marian's voice before she even saw her. The villagers of Sherwood were temporarily living at Egret Village since the sheriff had had their homes burned. Thanks to King Richard, the village had begun its restoration, but it would take a while until it was completed.

Belle pushed open the door of a small cottage and caught sight of Marian treating a woman's burned arm.

"He was the sweetest," the woman gushed

CHAPTER 5

as Marian gently rubbed a cream on her burns. "One time, I dropped my food on the way home from the market. Robin jumped right down from his horse and insisted on carrying the heavy sacks of vegetables all the way back to my home. He's such a selfless, caring young man."

"All done," Marian said with a smile. She helped the older woman to her feet. "Only a few more treatments and your arm should be fully healed."

"Thank you, sweetheart." The woman pinched Marian's cheek and smiled. "Now I see why our Robin was so smitten with you."

Marian's face reddened and she averted her eyes so as not to give the nice lady the wrong idea. The rumor about Marian having to kiss Robin in order to save his life had spread around the village like wildfire, and Belle couldn't even imagine the pressure she must've been feeling. Truth was that no one knew what had happened to Robin, or to where he'd been taken. Or what that whole idea of a true love's kiss even meant.

"Make sure not to lift any weight on that arm, okay?"

The woman started to walk away but then stopped and stood there in silence for a few seconds. "Is it true that only true love's kiss will bring our Robin back?" she asked, turning back around to look at Marian.

"I don't know," Marian said, her voice soft and empathetic. "But I'm sure Will and Red will get to the bottom of it, and you'll have him back in no time."

"Will you help them?" the woman asked. "Or at least try?"

Marian nodded. "I will do what I can," she said. "But from what I've heard, he's survived worse threats without me. I'm sure he'll pull through this one too."

The woman smiled at the reassurance. "Thank you."

Marian smiled. "You're welcome."

Belle opened the door wider and stepped aside to let the woman step out before entering Marian's humble home.

"Belle!" Marian beamed, coming to give her friend a hug. "What a nice surprise."

"I see the village has heard about the true love's kiss," Belle said, closing the door behind her.

CHAPTER 5

Marian rolled her eyes. "And somehow they think I'm the one who's going to save him," she said, taking a seat and waving for Belle to follow. "Clearly, they have all been suckered into believing that cursed book."

Belle knew exactly what book Marian was referring to. Many years ago, a man came from another realm through the Mirror of Reason, and he somehow knew so much about the Chanted Forest and the people living in it. He had books about them. He even gave Robin a book that told a story about him and Marian ending up together. He had also given Belle a book.

"You haven't read it yet, have you?" Belle asked, removing her cloak and taking a seat across from her friend. "Trust me, I didn't want to read mine either."

Marian narrowed her eyes. "What did yours say?"

"Mine was wrong," Belle muttered, discreetly brushing a finger over the scar on her arm. The scar from the alpha that turned her into a wolf. Somehow, she'd become the beast of her own story. "Anyway, I need your help with something if not too much trouble."

Marian leaned forward, curious. "Anything. You know that."

Belle dug into her satchel and pulled out the glass vial with Nathaniel's blood inside. "I need you to test this blood for me." She handed Marian the vial. "I need to know if there are any chemicals in it."

"What are you looking for?" Marian asked, lifting the vial and holding it up to inspect the crimson liquid.

"Anything that would cause... memory loss."

Marian's brows creased with concern. "Should I be worried?" she asked, looking as if she was ready to pounce on Belle to check her pupils. "Belle, you would tell me if you were suffering from memory loss, right?"

"I'm not," Belle assured her. "That's not my blood. It's for a friend. I promise."

Marian let out a sigh of relief, then smiled. "You scared me there for a second. Well, make yourself at home. I'll go take a look at this for you." She got up and walked across the room. The small kitchen was in the corner, divided only by an island counter.

Belle watched Marian, wondering how

much she knew about what had happened to Nathaniel. Did she know that Prince John had kept him in a dungeon? Could she have helped Emmett in getting rid of her brother? Belle didn't think Marian was capable of such evil, but if that wasn't the case, then why didn't she ever tell Belle about him?

Regardless of her intentions, Marian kept her brother a secret for a reason, and as much as Belle wanted to come clean and tell her friend that Nathaniel was safe and staying at her house, Belle was afraid of what Marian might do. At the very least, she would insist on seeing him. Perhaps she would even want to bring him home. If she did that, there was no hiding him from Emmett, and that would put Nathaniel's life at risk. Or worse, his freedom. If Emmett didn't kill him, he would most likely have him locked up again. Belle couldn't bring herself to risk it. Nathaniel had been through enough already. He just needed some time to heal.

"So, I heard the beast came out again last night," Marian said, turning the fire on top of the stove. "It was further south, but still, even though the people here are getting used to wolves because of Will and his pack being seen around these parts, they're terrified of the beast."

"I can't blame them. I'm a wolf and *I'm* afraid of that beast," Belle confessed, even though her fear never stopped her from facing him or protecting the villages. "I've seen the aftermath of his slaughter. He's heartless."

"And yet, you keep running after him." Marian knew her friend well. "Will keeps saying that if he hears of you doing that again, he's going to put you in his pack."

Her little brother was so protective, bless his heart. But she didn't belong to a pack. She didn't even belong as a wolf. And as soon as Nathaniel got the cure ready, the wolf inside of her would be gone and she would go back to being human.

"I don't run *after* him," Belle clarified. "I just try to keep the people safe. He's killed too many already."

"All the more reason to be careful, Belle," Marian asked, giving her friend a stern look. "The stories I've heard are horrific. He isn't like other wolves."

"I am being careful," Belle said, knowing that wasn't a joking matter.

"Then what happened last night?" Marian asked, putting a pot of water over the fire, then turning to look at Belle. "With the beast."

Belle cocked her head, wondering how Marian knew she had gone after the beast. Marian smiled, then pointed to Belle's arm. A fresh wound scarred her skin. Probably from one of the villagers with a sword when she pushed through them.

She looked back at Marian with a sigh. "Please, don't tell Will."

"I'm just afraid for you," Marian admitted.

"I know. But that's exactly why I need to know who he is. If we know his human form, it'll be so much easier to catch him. And I'm so close."

Marian reached for a dumbosie plant inside a jar, then pulled out a couple of petals. "How close?" she asked, dropping the petals inside the boiling water, then looking into the pot to examine it.

Belle rose to her feet, then rushed to her

friend with eager eyes. "I heard his voice last night."

Marian looked away from the pot with eyes widened as Belle leaned over the island counter. "Did you recognize the voice?"

Belle nodded. "Yes and no."

Marian stared at Belle, confused. "Which is it?"

Belle shook her head. "It sounded familiar, but I can't remember where I heard his voice before, and it didn't help that it sounded muffled like he was underwater or something."

"Any ideas of who it could be?"

"No clue," Belle confessed. "But I almost got into his head last night."

Marian shook her head as she let a single drop of blood fall into the water, then turned to her friend with a frown. "I don't like that one bit."

Belle reached for her friend's hand over the counter and gave it an encouraging squeeze. "I know it's scary, but don't worry. If I ever catch him, I'll call for the pack."

"Promise?"

Belle offered her a soft smile. "Promise. Now, you wanna hear something strange?"

"Sure, because everything up until now hasn't been strange at all," Marian teased.

Belle chuckled, then bit her lip, remembering what she noticed the night before.

"Okay, so, last night... the beast didn't attack anyone. He raided people's homes the same way he's been doing for a while, but I think it's the first time he didn't harm anyone."

"Maybe you got there in time," Marian suggested, turning back to examine the water.

"I also noticed that he jumped out of a house with a bag in his mouth," Belle said, tapping a finger to her lips as she searched her memories for more details. "It's as if he was looking for something."

"That being said, I think I got something," Marian said, peering into the pot.

Belle walked around the counter to stand next to Marian in the kitchen, where Marian stood over a pot of boiling water. "What is it?"

Marian stepped aside to let Belle take a look. The boiling water had a single petal of a dumbosie plant floating at the top. Belle watched as the plant changed from a pale white to a glowing blue.

"What's happening?" Belle asked. "Why is it changing color?"

"Because of this…" Marian reached for the rest of the blood that was still inside the vile and repeated the process in front of Belle. She let a few drops fall into the water and immediately, as the blood dissolved, the water began to glow a bright blue. After a few seconds, the dumbosie petal absorbed its color and also began to glow. "If the blood is contaminated in any way, the dumbosie petal will absorb everything except for the blood itself. So, this glow…" She turned to meet her friend's eyes. "There's definitely something in it."

"Any idea what it could be?" Belle asked.

Marian looked into the pot again, the blue glow reflecting against her skin. "Dumbosies only ever glow like this when near mermaid scales."

"Mermaid scales?" Belle echoed, watching as Marian pulled away and took the pot off the fire. "How could that end up in someone's bloodstream?"

"While on Pearl Island, I saw medicine containing oils from mermaid's scales,"

Marian explained. "I had no idea they could be extracted, but it's mostly used as a hallucinogen to help people endure the pain during a procedure."

"A hallucinogen?" Belle touched her lips thoughtfully. Maybe that would explain the connection to Nathaniel's memory loss. The hallucinogen in his blood could have been affecting his mind. Could Emmett have done that too? For his brother to forget his own identity. To forget that he was the rightful heir to the throne. Emmett wouldn't have known that much about medicine. And Prince John didn't have the resources to capture mermaids. Only the King of Shores was known to successfully capture mermaids, but he would never have dealings with that despicable Prince. They were rivals. So, where else would he have acquired the scales?

"Have you ever seen this used to erase someone's memory?" Belle asked.

"No, it would have to be an overdose for this hallucinogen to have an effect like that," Marian replied.

Belle watched Marian for any sign of nervousness. If she knew what had been done to Nathaniel, her pressure would rise and her pulse would race, but as Belle listened for a fast heartbeat, there was none. It was normal. She wasn't lying.

"Who does Prince John have alliances with?" Belle asked, still watching Marian.

"Other than my brother," Marian said, "the only other familiar face I've seen around the palace while I was there was Aria."

"Aria?" Belle echoed, surprised. "She's allied herself with him?"

"I don't know what business they've made together," Marian confessed. "But she came around quite a bit while I was there."

Belle gazed toward the fluorescent water once more. Aria's face surfaced in her mind. "She does have a mermaid stone necklace," Belle murmured.

"What does that mean?" Marian asked.

Belle looked at her friend. "It means... she has a lot of explaining to do."

#

Belle entered The Snow Queen's gate, but as she walked toward the castle door, Belle heard someone whistling in the garden. She walked around the frozen lake and followed the sound until she spotted Snow, Aria's sister, by a fountain in the center of the garden.

As Belle approached, she noticed Snow whispering to an owl who rested on her arm. Snow had the ability to communicate with animals, which was quite fascinating to Belle. Once the owl flew away, Snow swung around.

"Belle!" Snow beamed, coming to give her a hug. "It's so good to see you."

"You too." Belle enveloped Snow in a tight embrace. "So, did the owl have anything interesting to report?"

"That's my Roger," Snow added with a proud smile. "He's actually quite the collector." Snow lifted an old compass that looked a lot like something Belle's father would've owned. "He always comes back with something every time I send him out to check the perimeters of the castle."

"What is he checking for?"

Snow glanced toward the castle with a distasteful expression. "Since my sister became The *Snow Queen*..." She enunciated the title with disdain. "She's made a lot of enemies.

So, I try to keep the animals on lookout in case we're attacked."

"If anything does happen, reach out to Will," Belle said. "The pack could be here in no time."

Snow seemed surprised. "They would help The Snow Queen?"

"They wouldn't do it for her," Belle said. "But they would come for you."

Snow flashed a grateful smile. "Thank you, but... I wouldn't accept the pack's help."

Belle was taken aback. "Why not?"

"Because if it means ending the rule of The Snow Queen," Snow replied. "I would gladly open the gates myself."

"Oh, Snow. You don't mean that."

Snow gave Belle a serious look. "She killed the love of my life, Belle. That is unforgivable." When her eyes filled with tears, she looked away and touched her necklace. Belle wondered if George had given it to her.

"You may not know this, but..." She paused, hoping Snow would turn around, but she didn't. "When your sister thought you had died alongside your parents, I have never seen Aria cry so much. She wept for weeks."

CHAPTER 5

When Snow didn't respond, Belle put an encouraging hand on her shoulder. "Despite the bad decisions she's made... your sister loves you very much."

"The Snow Queen is not my sister," Snow said firmly, finally turning around to meet Belle's eyes. "She's an evil person who needs to be dethroned, and I will support whoever challenges that."

"You know..." Belle added, keeping her voice soft. "Sometimes people do bad things for good reason."

Belle didn't understand Aria's dramatic personality shift either, but she knew Aria. All the horrors she had to endure and the years she spent in hiding, living with Robin as an outlaw. It wasn't easy, but none of that ever changed her. She was still the same old Aria. Feisty but full of heart. Whatever had happened to make her take the place of The Evil Queen must've left her with no choice. To everyone else, she'd turned into a villain, but Belle knew there must've been more to the story and refused to believe her friend had turned into a cold-blooded killer for no good reason. Somewhere beneath the frosty exterior was the fiercely loyal Aria.

Snow stared at Belle for a long time, then offered a small smile. "I don't know how you do it, but you always give the best advice."

Belle smiled, giving Snow's shoulder a light squeeze. "Everything is going to be okay. I'm sure of it." Belle couldn't have been sure of anything, but her father always taught her that hope was the brightest light to a dark road.

Snow nodded. "So, what brings you here? What do you want from Aria?"

Belle pulled back and took a seat on a stone bench nearby. The sky was clear, and the spring breeze was cool on her skin. "I was hoping she could tell me more about her mermaid necklace. Is she around?"

"Looking for me?" Aria's voice came from above and Belle looked up.

Aria stood tall and regal in a floor-length, royal blue gown. White feathers covered the hemline of the dress, and she had fashioned her blonde hair to sit in a tight knot on the back of her head. She stood on a patio on the second floor, looking down. Snow furrowed her brows at the sight of her sister, then turned on her heels and walked away, giving Belle a small farewell.

Aria let out a long breath as she watched her sister disappear into the garden, then looked at Belle. "What can I do for you?" Her words were unusually formal, and it was hard to believe this was the same Aria she had helped in the manor just months ago.

"Your mermaid necklace," Belle said, looking up at Aria. "May I see it?"

"First, I have a question for you," Aria began. "What do you know about the genie bracelet?"

It took Belle a few seconds to remember what bracelet Aria was referring to. While visiting with her a while back, The Evil Queen's guards raided the manor and locked a bracelet on Aria's wrist which made her incapable of using her powers. "You mean the one that suppressed your powers?" Belle asked, just to be sure.

Aria nodded. "Yes, do you know where it might be?"

Belle cocked her head, confused. "I thought Jack had the bracelet?"

"He sold it for safe passage to the Ice

Mountains," Aria explained. "Now, tell me. Do you have any idea who might've wanted it?"

Belle thought about it for a long moment, then looked up at the Queen again. "The whole kingdom, if it means suppressing your powers."

Aria winced. "That's what I was afraid of," she muttered, but Belle's keen hearing could detect even the faintest of whispers.

"I'll let you know if I hear of anything. Now, I need your help with something else," Belle said, and though Aria didn't respond, she waited for Belle to continue. "Your mermaid necklace. Can I see it?"

"Sorry to disappoint," Aria replied, touching her bare collarbone and chewing her lip. "I no longer possess the necklace."

Belle couldn't help but sense the irritation in her voice. Part of her wished the two of them could go somewhere quiet, like the library, and have a more frank conversation. But Belle needed to help Nathaniel, so whatever Aria's problems were, they would have to wait.

CHAPTER 5

"Where is it?" she asked, eyeing Aria carefully.

"I traded it for a mirror shard," Aria said.

"To whom?"

Aria scowled as if remembering the day. "A blasted mermaid with the most infuriating giggle. Her name is Lexa."

Belle brought a finger to her lips, thoughtfully. "Where do I find that mermaid?"

"Pirate Cove," Aria said. "She has a cave of junk off the coast, but if you want anything from her, be sure to have something to offer in return."

"And *how* do I find her?"

Aria met Belle's eyes for a moment, and she gave her a piercing stare. "She'll find you."

CHAPTER 6

Nathaniel

Nathaniel tried to focus on his research papers as he read the first page for the hundredth time and not pay attention to the soft moans coming from the other room.

Will and Red were nice enough to him, but the two of them acted like they were on their honeymoon. When they sat in the same room for dinner, Nathaniel couldn't ignore the way Will looked at Red like he was ready to throw the bowl of stew aside and devour her on the table. Meanwhile, Red's cheeks were often stained pink and her lips plump.

Being alone with the two lovebirds was a unique form of torture to Nathaniel, but at times, he found himself wanting to remember if there was ever a woman in his life. But there wasn't any. Except for Belle.

He would be lying if he told himself that he never noticed how beautiful she was. As much as he enjoyed having Will and Red around, he couldn't deny that he missed Belle while she was gone. And in that moment, he decided that if she ever left again, he would go with her.

On the third afternoon, Nathaniel decided to shave his beard. He took off his shirt and sharpened a blade. It wasn't until he was done that he spotted Belle walking up the garden path. He had never been so happy to see a person. He didn't even bother to put on his shirt before he raced out to meet her with a broad grin.

"Wow, am I glad to see you back," he said, dragging a hand through his thick hair with a sigh. "Those two can't keep their hands off each other. It's been quite distracting." He chuckled but stopped when he noticed Belle's eyes had widened. She was looking at his bare chest and her cheeks grew pink. Nathaniel wasn't sure whether to be embarrassed or flattered.

"You shaved," she noted, her voice breaking. "It looks nice. And you're healing very well—I mean, fast. Very fast." She cleared her throat and Nathaniel suppressed a grin. He had eaten more than his fair share of meat, and due to Red and Will's antics, he had been working out in the barn to get away.

Push-ups were easy for him, and judging by his muscular physique, he reasoned that he must have spent many hours a day exercising in his cell.

"Did you find what you were looking for?" he asked.

Will and Red must have heard, because they appeared from the side of the cabin and ran to join them.

"Did you see Marian? Any news on Robin?" Red asked in a breathy voice as she caught up.

Belle's smile didn't reach her eyes. "Yes… and no. But let's go inside. I'll explain everything over dinner." Belle walked into the cabin, bidding everyone to follow, and she remained tight-lipped about her trip while she prepared an onion soup.

Nathaniel didn't want to press her when she was tired after a long journey, but the longer he waited for her to talk, the harder it was to stay quiet.

Finally, as everyone sat down to eat, Nathaniel leaned forward and looked at Belle. "So, what did you find?"

"I don't want you to be alarmed, but..." Belle clasped her hands and rested her forehead on them. "Marian found oil from mermaid scales in your blood."

The kitchen fell quiet and everyone at the table stared at Belle like she had spoken a foreign language.

"What does that mean?" Will asked. "Is he part-mermaid or something?"

Red snorted in her hand, but Belle gave the both of them a reproachful look before turning back to Nathaniel. "No. It just means you've been given a high dose of hallucinogen. So, whoever did this to you not only wanted your memories gone but wanted to make you vulnerable."

Nathaniel straightened his back and wanted to retort that he was anything but vulnerable. But the truth was, even without the oil from mermaid scales in his blood, he had no memories, and that was a weakness whether he liked it or not.

"I've arranged to meet a mermaid so we could get more answers," Belle added, picking up her drink.

Nathaniel nodded along. "I'm coming with you."

Belle met his determined stare and opened her mouth, but then her brows pinched, and she shut it again, changing her mind. "Fine. We leave first thing in the morning."

Nathaniel shifted his weight on the saddle of Philly, Belle's horse, and grimaced. He didn't enjoy the sensation that he was sliding to one side and would have much preferred to walk or take Belle's carriage.

But that would've drawn too much attention, and they were trying to be discreet. He glanced at the golden wolf strolling alongside him, apparently unaware of his misgivings.

What it must be like to be a wolf, he thought. From his papers, it appeared that he had a lifelong interest in wolves, and even without his memories, he couldn't help but find them fascinating. So, why would he have been so involved in finding them a cure? Perhaps it made sense then, but at that moment, he just couldn't fathom why a wolf would even *want* to be cured?

Belle alone was stronger than a group of men. She had a sense of smell more powerful than a black bear and the hearing of a bat. Then there was the telepathy.

The wolf's ear twitched, and Nathaniel smiled, wondering if Belle could read his thoughts as easily as she could her brother's. But then two yellow eyes looked up at him and he lurched back, nearly falling off the horse at the intensity of her stare. Was it sadness behind those eyes? He wasn't sure, but feeling her gaze on him did something funny to his stomach. He grabbed the reins more tightly and looked at the path ahead.

After a few seconds, Nathaniel looked down, but the wolf had disappeared. He whipped his head from left to right. She was gone, leaving him alone in the dusty path. Nathaniel slowed the horse and jumped down, happy to be back on solid ground. He was just tying the reins to a tree when Belle returned, now in human form and fully dressed.

"Aria told me to bring something to exchange," Belle said, reaching around Nathaniel to rummage in one of the bags hanging from the saddle. "Apparently, the mermaid collects human objects, so I thought this would be perfect."

A gust of salty air shot toward him, blowing strands of Belle's dark hair across her face. He resisted the urge to close his eyes and bathe in her warm scent picked up by the breeze. Instead, he kept his expression neutral and watched as Belle fastened the ties on her shirt.

Belle was still talking to him, but he couldn't hear a word. He simply watched her full lips moving, making his pulse beat against his eardrums like a line of guards marching. He clenched his jaw, trying to ignore it.

Nathaniel swallowed as her scent grew more intense and her arm brushed against him. He looked away from her, but Belle hummed in his ear as she struggled to find whatever this mystery gift was, and Nathaniel's nostrils flared. As if a bolt of lightning struck his brain, he tensed as a rush of adrenaline coursed through his whole body. He bit back against the sudden urge to reach for Belle and wrap his arms around her.

His eyes found her lips again, and he suddenly wondered what they might feel like to touch. Would they be as soft and velvety as they looked? The desire came seemingly from nowhere and took him entirely by surprise. Belle stepped back, shattering his thoughts, and Nathaniel mentally shook himself. His whole body tingled as she looked at him with a pair of big brown eyes.

"Found it!" She held up a music box with a couple dancing a waltz and flashed him a beaming smile. "Do you think she'll like it?"

Nathaniel blinked several times, looking at the rusted music box as his stupor fizzled away.

"Sure," he said with a nod, hoping she wouldn't notice how his voice sounded like a strangled cry. He cleared his throat and furrowed his brows. "So, you said this mermaid lives in a cave?"

Belle gave him an odd smile before shaking her head. "Her father is Poseidon, King of the Sea. The cave is just where she keeps her collection."

They walked in silence, following the winding path toward the beach as it narrowed, forcing them closer together. Nathaniel clenched his jaw as Belle's arm hovered barely an inch from his, her warmth radiating over him like the noontime sun.

Finally, the sound of ocean waves took over the ringing in Nathaniel's ears, and they emerged from the forest to a beach. Golden beams of sunlight scattered across the surface of the water like millions of glittering jewels. It was a stark contrast to the muddy brown sand mingled with stones along the shoreline. Dead leaves crunched beneath his boots as he followed Belle to the beach. They stopped at the shoreline, looking out at the calm waters. In the distance was a dark cove in the middle of the sea with nothing but a line of jagged rocks leading to it.

Nathaniel stopped and scratched the back of his neck, trying to remember if he knew how to swim. As he looked down, nudging a rock in the damp sand, the salty smell of seaweed flooded his senses.

Belle's hand rested on his arm, and it sent a bolt of hot energy straight to his heart. He turned to meet her worried gaze, and the sea breeze washed over him, smothering him in the smell of spices. The palms of his hands grew sweaty as he wondered what had gotten into him. All of these feelings swirled inside him like a cyclone. He blinked several times, gazing into Belle's eyes, worried he might drown in them.

Then, she blinked and looked away. If she had him under a trance, it broke as she let go of him and pointed to the ocean.

"There she is," Belle whispered. "Isn't she the most beautiful creature you've ever seen?"

Nathaniel kept his eyes on Belle. The length of her hair flowed back as the sea breeze washed over her face. He stared as her pair of rose-red lips parted then curved upward. "Yes," he said finally. "The most beautiful of all."

Belle waved, and Nathaniel finally noticed the mermaid swimming toward them. "Hi, there."

Bobbing in the water was a dark-haired mermaid. Her magnificent fin stuck out like a fan of glittering diamonds and her milky skin had an unearthly glow to it. Her dark eyes fixed on Belle for a moment. "Are you Belle?"

"Yes," Belle replied. "And this is my friend Nathaniel."

The mermaid's gaze flitted to Nathaniel. "It's not every day I get summoned by The Snow Queen." Her voice was soft and musical. Nathaniel couldn't help but smile at the sound.

"Are you friends with Aria?" Belle asked.

"I wouldn't say *friends*," Lexa replied. "But there have been advantages in allying with her."

Belle nipped her bottom lip, and suddenly Nathaniel couldn't take his eyes off her again. There could've been one hundred mermaids in the water, it wouldn't have made any difference to him.

"Aria said you need my help?" Lexa asked, snapping him out of his head.

Belle's cheeks reddened, and Nathaniel wondered if this was the first time she had admitted she couldn't do everything on her own. "I was wondering if you could tell us more about your mermaid scales."

Nathaniel looked back at the mermaid just in time to see her swim back with her brows raised, as though Belle's question had struck her like a bolt of lightning.

"What makes you think I'm at liberty to share that information?" she asked curtly.

Nathaniel and Belle exchanged looks.

"I brought you something," Belle said, shoving into her satchel and pulling out the music box. "This is for you."

Lexa's eyes widened. "What is it?" she asked, intrigued.

Belle twisted heart shaped iron on the side and the couple began to spin into a waltz with an angelic melody. Lexa watched the couple dancing with eyes unblinking.

"It's for you," Belle said. "I just need some information."

Lexa arched a skeptical brow, but then

stretched out her open palms. "What would you want to know?"

Belle handed Lexa the music box. "Traces of the oil from a mermaid scale were found in Nathaniel's blood," she explained, her voice wavering. "We were hoping you could tell us about the effects of the hallucinogen."

Lexa's mouth narrowed to a thin line as she hummed in thought. "How did this come about?"

"I was a prisoner," Nathaniel responded. "But that's all I remember. My memory is gone.

"And he's had blackouts," Belle added. She didn't turn to meet his eyes. Lexa, on the other hand, gave him a curious look.

"Please…" Belle knelt at the water's edge. "Whatever information you can share, it would be tremendously helpful."

Nathaniel crouched beside her, intrigued.

Lexa glanced over her shoulder, then leaned in closer to Belle. "Mermaids have the ability of mind control," she explained. "Our voices can hypnotize, while the sight of our scales can cause illusions. If your friend really does have a drop of that in his blood, he can easily be mind-controlled."

"How is that even possible?" Nathaniel asked, leaning in as if waiting for a secret.

Lexa frowned. "Much is possible with a mermaid stone," she replied. "If your blood is mixed with the oil and sprinkled on a mermaid stone, then whoever has that stone could potentially have full control over you."

Nathaniel could feel his blood draining from his face. "Does that mean…?"

"Yes." Lexa inclined her head with a frown. "Someone has been controlling you."

Belle looked at Nathaniel with wide eyes.

He swallowed again and tried to ignore the jitters in his stomach. "Prince John was controlling me…" he muttered in a hollow voice. "But what for?"

As if the words unlocked a dark corner of his mind, Nathaniel dropped on rocky ground as a memory flashed before his eyes…

A filthy underground room with medical equipment scattered across a desk along with papers of formulae and wolf diagrams. Then a threatening growl sent the hairs on the back of his neck on end. He turned around with a needle in his hand, only to catch a pair of crimson eyes glowing in front of him. The beast growled again as he grew into something unnatural right before Nathaniel's eyes. The creature stood on his hind legs, his size was like that of a grizzly. Nathaniel's pulse raced, followed by a piercing howl...

Nathaniel lay with his cheek pressed to the dark sand. The tide wet his hair as it flowed inward, then a pair of hands gripped his shoulders and rolled him around.

"Nathaniel, can you hear me?" Belle hovered over him with concern in her big, brown eyes.

Nathaniel pressed his eyes shut, then shook his head. The sun was too bright, and his head was pounding. "I think I had a memory," he muttered, pushing himself to sit up.

"That's good, though, right?" Belle looked at Lexa for confirmation, but when she narrowed her eyes and studied Nathaniel, he knew something was wrong.

"If what you say is true, and he does have oil from mermaid scales in his blood, then it'll be hard to discern what's a real memory and what's a hallucination," Lexa explained, but not too quietly that Nathaniel could not hear.

Belle sucked in a breath but kept her hand

on his shoulder. Her warmth burned right to his soul.

"How do we remove the hallucinogen from his system?" Belle asked, shifting her attention back to Lexa.

"You can't. It's part of his blood now. The only way to break free from a mermaid's trance is if his mind regains consciousness on its own. It's rare, but not impossible," Lexa replied. "As for his memories... you can have him drink the water from the Reditus Cave. Just be careful with Neri. She's not trustworthy."

"Thank you, Lexa, for all your help."

"No, thank you both. If Prince John really is responsible for this, then I must make haste and speak to my father," Lexa said with an urgent tone. "We must find out who provided him with such information. Mind-control cannot fall into the wrong hands. Farewell, friends."

A splash followed and a light trickle of water fell over Nathaniel as he pushed himself to stand. His heart beat so fast, he could hear it pulsing in his ears. Belle's worried face appeared into view.

"What did you see?" she asked, grasping his arms as if trying to steady him.

Nathaniel looked out at the sparkling sea. Seagulls flew in the sunny sky. He clenched his jaw and looked back at Belle, his eyes widening at his realization.

"Prince John didn't use me to poison his brother," he said, the words cutting the back of his throat like daggers. "He used me to create the beast."

CHAPTER 7

Belle

$\mathcal{A}$ spray of light rain fell between the tree branches as Belle walked alongside Nathaniel while he rode her horse. Being in her wolf form made for a quiet trip back through the forest. Though even if she was in human form, she wasn't sure he was in the mood to talk. She looked up and caught him looking at her.

He looked away quickly, and she brushed her snout against his leg, hoping he would say something. Even though she couldn't respond, or communicate telepathically with him, she could still listen if he wanted to talk.

He looked down at her again, and their eyes met. "Don't try to make me feel better," he muttered. "I don't deserve it."

She brushed his leg again, not sure how else to comfort him. It wasn't his fault. He had been manipulated to create the beast, and it made sense. With a killer on the loose, Prince John could charge the people extra taxes in order to provide hunters to guard the villages. It was all about money with him. And power. Even though she hadn't known Nathaniel long, he didn't seem like the type of person who would ever agree to such an evil scheme. He was kind and wore his heart on his sleeve. She could see in his eyes the guilt and remorse eating him inside, and it killed her not to be able to soothe his pain.

The sound of a twig breaking under a heavy boot caught Belle's attention, and her ears pricked up. She crouched to the ground, then squinted into the distance. There was no one in sight, which could only mean the sound came from afar. She sniffed the air, searching for a scent.

CHAPTER 7

"What's wrong?" Nathaniel asked.

The distinct smell of mud filled her senses, and she immediately realized who was watching her.

She jumped back and snarled in the direction of the sound. When nothing came into view, she bit into a loose branch on the ground then swung it in the air. It hit the ground with a thud, followed by the loud snap of a bear trap.

Belle howled, challenging the hunters to show themselves. A sword flew by, grazing her skin. She yelped and jumped to the side. But then the swoosh of an arrow came from her left, and she leapt in the air, knocking Nathaniel down from the horse. A sharp pain shot up her leg and an ear-splitting cry ripped through her throat.

They dropped to the ground with a loud thud as the arrow stuck out of her leg. She grabbed the arrow with her teeth and pulled it out with a hard yank. By the time she looked at Nathaniel, his eyes were rolling back. Blood dripped from his forehead, and a surge of panic rippled through her. She bit at his cloak and threw the hood over his head to make sure no one saw his face, then she lifted him in the air and propped him back on the horse, slumping him face down and unconscious. As heavy boots ran in their direction, she swung her tail against the hind of her horse, and the animal galloped into the woods, headed away from the footsteps.

Belle darted toward the hunters in order to keep them from following Nathaniel, but the sound of heavy boots suddenly stopped. Two hunters that were coming from behind her stopped running, and she sniffed the air. The scent of more hunters hit her nostrils, and it grew stronger with every step. She kept running toward them so that Nathaniel could escape. Even though he wasn't a wolf, he was a prince. And one who'd been missing for years. The ransom they would get on him would set those hunters for life.

Suddenly, the rough texture of a rope wrapped around her paw, a snap echoed in the woods, and the world turned upside down. She hung from a tree, ten feet above the ground. She tried biting the rope, but pain in her leg made it difficult to push herself up.

She closed her eyes and focused her

CHAPTER 7

thoughts on her brother. Calling to him. Begging to be heard. But there was no response. Had she been part of the pack, their thoughts would've been connected, and he would've heard her immediately. But she had asked to leave. To be set free. To follow her own path. And now, she was alone. Caught in a trap.

She howled to the skies, but this time it came out as a strangled cry. A man stepped out from behind a tree with green leaves attached to his clothes as camouflage.

"Looks like it's our lucky day, boys," the hunter cheered. Five young men stepped into view, surrounding her. Some looked scared, others excited. They were in training, which meant there was still a chance she could escape.

She focused on the hunter who had a smile on his face. He must've been the leader. The trainer. The only professional in the group. He pulled out a knife from his sheath, then pointed at one of the young men.

"You…" he called out. "What do we do next?"

The young man's gulps echoed in Belle's

hypersensitive hearing. Even his heart began to race as his eyes locked with hers. "We... uh... kill it?"

The hunter grunted in frustration. "*How* do we kill it?" He pointed his knife to another young man. "You."

"A cut on the neck," the other young man answered. "Then let them bleed out."

Belle winced at the thought. She'd seen many wolves be slaughtered this way, and the memories burned inside her mind like a nightmare she couldn't shake. Maybe if they knew wolves were part human, they wouldn't treat them like that. Or maybe not. After all, Emmett had seen a child shift in front of him once and still tried to kill him while in wolf form.

When had those hunters lost their humanity?

"According to King Emmett's decree, will the reward be larger for a dead wolf or a live one?" one of the trainees asked, clearly seeing the wolf hanging in front of him as the solution to his financial troubles.

"I've heard he's looking for one particular

wolf," another trainee cut in. "But he'll repay us either way."

"What if we don't want to kill?" the hunter asked, pointing at yet another of his trainees.

"We make sure they can't run," the young man said, nocking an arrow in his bow and aiming it at Belle's other leg. She tried yanking her legs from the rope, only to have it tighten around her paws even more. She bared her teeth and reached for the rope with even more desperation than before.

"Do it now!" the hunter ordered, and the young man released it. The whistle of the arrow cut through the air, and Belle closed her eyes, bracing herself for the excruciating impact of the arrow piercing through her flesh.

But it never came.

Instead, she could hear the beat of their hearts racing with fear. Belle opened her eyes to see what had them so shaken up. A wolf stood on his hind legs, blocking her from the group of hunters. The arrow that was meant for her ended up on the ground, broken to pieces.

"What is *that*?" one of the young men asked, his voice shaking.

"Whatever it is," another young man replied, his voice also trembling with fear, "it's *not* a wolf."

Looking at him from behind, Belle noticed his shoulders were wider than his waist, and his arms stronger than his legs. He stood taller and bigger than any wolf Belle had ever seen.

It was the *beast*.

A sword flew in his direction, and he knocked it to the ground. He thrashed his head toward the hunter who had thrown it and snarled.

"Run!" the hunter commanded, and the group of young men couldn't disperse fast enough.

The beast arched its back and roared so loud, the ground trembled and birds flew from the trees and into the misty clouds. But to Belle's surprise, the beast didn't follow after the hunters. Instead, he turned around and came face to face with her still hanging from the tree. For a moment, she wished the hunter's arrow had pierced her heart and killed her on the spot. It would've been a much more peaceful death than this.

The beast locked his crimson eyes on hers, then pulled back his front leg, snapping his claws into view. Belle flinched and braced herself for the fatal strike. The beast swung his paw above her head, and in the blink of an eye, she dropped to the ground with a thud. She winced as her wound scraped on a tree root, but quickly staggered to her feet, biting back the pain.

She grimaced as she stepped back with her injured leg. *Who are you?* she asked with her mind.

The beast stared at her without responding.

Why did you save me? she pressed. *I know a lot about you.*

The beast cocked its head with a sudden recognition. *You know nothing.*

Belle felt goosebumps at hearing the sound of her own voice coming from the beast. Except there was a rumble to her tone which echoed as if she was speaking from a cave. The beast was using her own voice to mask his own. That wasn't uncommon for wolves. If skilled enough, they could use the person's own voice, concealing their own to convey a message. She had done that many times before, but she never had anyone do it to her.

I know Nathaniel created you, she said.

And that was his biggest mistake, the beast responded with an edge in its tone. *Now, he'll deal with the consequences.*

Before Belle could say anything else, the beast disappeared into the woods. Even with Belle's sharp sight and keen sense of hearing, she lost him. She took a step forward, and a sharp pain shot up her leg. She winced. If the hunters came back, there was no way she would be able to run from them. She lifted her nose as the wind blew and caught a scent of her clothes nearby. They must've fallen from her horse as it galloped away with Nathaniel.

Nathaniel!

Belle pushed through the pain and hurried to get her clothes. Pain shot up her leg as she forced her pants over her injured leg, but she bit back the pain. She needed to find Nathaniel before anyone else did. Finding him while in human form would be a lot slower for Belle, but at least she knew where to look. Her horse's hooves left a clear trail in the muddy path, thanks to the rain.

She sniffed the air again, and when she caught Nathaniel's scent in the wind, a wave of relief washed over her.

Not only was he alive, but he wasn't too far away.

#

In human form, Belle sniffed the air for the millionth time. The sky had grown dark but at least the rain had stopped, and the earthy scent of her horse was stronger than ever. She was close.

She emerged from the forest and caught sight of a cave embedded in the side of a hill. She limped toward it, her strength fading with every step and longing for rest. Finally, she stopped at the mouth of the cave and whistled, listening for the sound of Philly's neigh. When she heard it, a wave of relief washed over her. A surge of adrenaline gave her renewed energy as she hurried inside, ignoring the stabbing pain that shot up her leg. Her horse towered over

Nathaniel's body as he laid immobile on the ground.

Belle hurried to his side and touched his shoulder. He moved with a grumble, and she let out another breath of relief.

"Oh, thank the heavens," she breathed, craning her neck to see his face as he rolled on his back. A small cut on his forehead wept tiny drops of blood along his temple. "Nathaniel, are you okay?"

"I'm fine," he replied, bringing a hand to his head, swiping the blood away with a grunt. But then he must've remembered what happened because his blue eyes shot open. "Are *you*?" He scanned her quickly, looking for any injuries. That was when his eyes locked on the large crimson stain on her pants. "Belle, you're bleeding."

"I'm fine." She put a protective arm over her thigh to keep him from touching her. "It's just a scratch."

He pushed himself to his knees, then gave her a pointed look. "Stubborn as a wolf."

"Am not!"

He motioned to her leg. "Then let me see."

Belle stared at him, debating whether or not to comply. It wasn't that she didn't trust him. She just wasn't used to anyone taking care of her. She spent most of her life taking care of herself and others. Accepting help from someone else was unnatural.

"Please?" he said, bringing her back from her thoughts. His eyes were gentle as he held her gaze. "I may not be a healer, but I know a thing or two about treating a wound."

She moved her arm hesitantly.

"Thank you," he said softly, then grabbed onto the fabric of her pants and ripped it apart. She winced and he frowned.

"Sorry."

Once the open gash was exposed, he examined it for a long moment. As a chill breeze blew past them, her wound began to itch.

"Wolves heal fast," she said in hopes that he would just leave it alone. But instead, his thumb began to gently caress the skin around her wound. She closed her eyes and let out a sigh of relief. It was soothing, and it helped with the itch.

"That may be true," he replied, keeping his voice soft, "but we still need to clean it."

"What?" She gulped loudly as her body tensed. "Okay, that's enough." She pushed his hands away, then crawled toward the wall and leaned against it. "I'll be fine."

Nathaniel arched a brow. "What are you so afraid of?"

She squared her shoulders, unwilling to admit it. "Nothing."

"In that case," he said, rising to his feet, "I'll be back."

"Wait, where are you going?" she asked tensely.

"To look for ingredients for a poultice," he said, but when his cut seeped again, he wiped the blood from his forehead with the sleeve of his cloak.

"You are not putting that disgusting goo on my leg."

He arched a curious brow. "And why not?"

She crossed her arms, then let out a murmur so low it came out almost like a grumble. "It burns."

Nathaniel suppressed a smile. "I never thought you would be afraid of a little burn."

"I'm not," she lied.

"Good," he said, slinging a bag on his shoulder. "Because it *is* going to burn. I'll be back."

"Wait—"

But he didn't listen. He left the cave. By the time he came back, she had lit the fire and propped her leg on a rolled-up blanket, wincing as the heat only made the pain worse. But she tried to cover up the pain as Nathaniel returned. He grabbed a waterskin from their bags, then rubbed the black paste on his hand. Belle frowned as he knelt in front of her.

"Please, be gentle," she pleaded.

Nathaniel's cheeks dimpled. "I'm always gentle." His tone was soft and caring, and a wave of warmth washed through her.

"Ready?" he asked, his voice still soft.

Belle took fistfuls of her cloak and braced herself, then she gave him a nod.

His gentle eyes stayed on her. "You could look away if you want to."

She shook her head quickly, still holding her breath.

He lifted the fabric of her cloak, exposing her bloody thigh. In the firelight, the skin around the wound was red and angry. He poured the water over it, washing away the congealed blood, and she winced against the searing pain. Nathaniel was true to his word. He drenched a cloth in water and dabbed her throbbing leg until all the blood had gone and the wound was clean. After he patted it dry with another rag, he gave her a quick glance, letting her know the worst was about to begin.

She watched with horror as he picked up a large leaf with black paste and scooped it out with his fingers. A stomach-churning aroma hit Belle when he drew closer with the poultice. As he gently rubbed it over the open gash, she grimaced then pressed her eyes shut. Maddening pain shot through her leg like a hot knife, but the sensation faded as quickly as it came, giving way to a throbbing ache.

"So, are you going to tell me what happened back there?" he asked, his thick brows rising as he gave her a careful look.

Belle knew he was just trying to distract her as he scooped more paste onto his fingers. "I should've picked up their scent," she grumbled as he smothered her wound and the burn spread through her thigh again. "That's what happens when I drop my guard."

"This wasn't your fault," Nathaniel assured her, the softness in his voice almost convincing her it was true. "These wolf hunters are getting more and more experienced."

"This was different," she said, opening her eyes with a thoughtful gaze toward the fire. "The arrow curved mid-air."

"What's so different about that?"

"Wolf hunters normally use traps and spears, not arrows," she explained. "Especially not arrows that curve."

She winced again and Nathaniel returned his attention to her wound.

"Sounds like you have a theory?" he asked.

She sat up on her forearms, still holding her cloak with balled fists as Nathaniel continued to work. "I only know one person who can curve an arrow like that," she said between breaths.

"And who's that?"

She gave him an annoyed look. "Are you done yet?"

"Almost," he replied, flashing her an

apologetic smile. He took the last of the paste, dragging his thumb along the edge, and the potent smell stifled her nose. Nathaniel didn't seem to notice. "Now, tell me. Who curves an arrow like no other?"

"Robin," she said, her reply echoing in the cave.

Nathaniel looked up to meet her eyes, shadows from the fire dancing against his skin. "Isn't that your brother's friend? I thought he was missing?"

"Not only that," she added. "But even if he wasn't missing, he would never shoot me. We're like family."

Nathaniel pulled back. "All done."

Belle looked at her cut. Thankfully, the burning had subsided. In a flash, she covered herself up with the cloak again and let out a shuddering breath of relief.

"It wasn't that bad, was it?"

"I guess not." She shrugged, trying to act nonchalant. "My dad always said that *more often than not, the worst pain is in the mind.*"

Nathaniel nodded. "Sounds like a wise man."

"Oh, he is." The thought of her father

brought a smile to her face, but sadness nipped at her insides. "And the most loving and caring man in the world."

"What about your mom?" he asked, sitting across from her and bringing the remnants of the black paste to the cut on his forehead.

"Here. Let me help," Belle offered, waving for him to come closer as she sat up.

He came to sit next to her and offered his hand. She scooped a bit of paste from his fingers, then turned toward him. His blue eyes were so close, and something fluttered inside her stomach. Ignoring the flutters, she pushed his hair up from his forehead, exposing his cut.

"Please be gentle," he teased.

She arched a taunting brow. "I'm never gentle."

He chuckled, and she suppressed a smile. When she rubbed the paste on his cut, he winced.

"Ouch." He pulled back. "You weren't kidding."

"Oh, please." She rolled her eyes. "Bring it here. I'm not done."

He drew closer and the movement toward her made it feel as if he was leaning in for a kiss. Even though he stopped midway, the thought suddenly filled her cheeks with heat.

"So, my mother…" she said, her mouth suddenly going dry. She focused on his cut again. "She died when I was little. Childbirth."

Nathaniel frowned as she continued to rub the paste on his cut. "I'm so sorry," he said softly.

"It's okay," she replied with a light shrug. "You can't really miss someone you never met, right?"

"Maybe not," he said. "But it still leaves a void."

Her eyes dropped to meet his, catching the reflection of the fire dancing in his eyes. The proximity made her cheeks burn again. "Do you remember your parents?"

He shook his head.

"Do you still feel a void?"

He nodded. "It's a different type of emptiness, but yes."

"I'm sorry." When she rubbed his cut again, she brushed a strand of hair from his face, almost like a caress. His eyes dropped to her lips and the flutters in her stomach spread across her body.

"All done." She turned away, afraid that the heat of the fire and the burning of the poultice would somehow be misinterpreted. It had to be the medicine. She was never vulnerable with anyone. She wiped her hand on her cloak as she returned to her place against the wall.

"Thank you," he said, pulling back. "How's your thigh?"

"Tingling, still," she replied, lifting her cloak to inspect the black paste smudged on her skin.

"It should go numb soon," Nathaniel said, examining her thigh.

Belle gave him a quizzical look. "How do you know that?"

"What?"

"If you don't have your memories, how do you know my wound should go numb soon? How did you even know about poultices?"

Nathaniel looked at the fire, deep in thought. "It wasn't a memory," he said in a low voice, then he lifted his eyes to meet her gaze. "It was knowledge."

"Knowledge?" Belle echoed.

"Yes. I mean... I just *knew* what it was and what it could do, even though there was no memory of me ever using it before." His face broke into a grin. "The mind is fascinating, isn't it?"

Belle watched as his eyes sparkled with intrigue. "Yes, it is," she agreed with a soft smile. "And if all goes well, tomorrow we'll meet Neri and this miraculous water she has and get your memories back. Now, *that* will be a lot more fascinating."

"Do you think it will go well?" he asked, slightly concerned.

"I like to believe it will."

He held her gaze for a long moment. "Then I trust you."

Her cheeks warmed again, and she looked away sheepishly. "Then trust me when I say we need a good night's rest," she added with a light chuckle. "Especially if..." She bit her bottom lip, then shook her head. "Never mind."

Nathaniel grabbed both of their bags that had fallen at the horse's feet. He tossed one behind him to rest his head on, then handed the other to Belle. By the time he laid down and turned on his side to face her, she was already lying on her back, staring at the firelight dancing across the jagged rocks above them.

"Especially if..." he said softly above the crackling of the fire. "What?"

Belle turned her head to look at him one last time. "If your memories *do* come back."

CHAPTER 8

Nathaniel

Flakes of snow fell like ash from the gray skies as Nathaniel and Belle navigated through the forest. They had been walking since sunrise, and after several hours, they reached a clearing with nothing more than an abandoned camp in the midst of several charred tree stumps. Nathaniel stopped to bend down and brush the light dusting of snow to reveal the scorched ground.

He looked up at Belle. "What happened here?"

Belle sighed heavily, and her eyes glazed over. "The Queen... was a real dragon." The corners of her mouth twitched as if she wanted to laugh but decided against it.

"I thought you said she had ice powers," Nathaniel said, brushing his hand on his pant leg as he came to a stand again.

Belle shook her head, stray hairs framing her face whipped from left to right, and at such close proximity, Nathaniel's nostrils became flooded in her natural scent. Now it was his turn to suppress a smile. But the horse neighed, jolting Nathaniel out of his daze.

"Not The Snow Queen," Belle corrected him as they carried on. Dead leaves crunched under their boots and the sound echoed in the quiet clearing. "The Evil Queen."

"The Chanted Forest sure is unlucky to have so many bad queens... I wonder what the next one will be. A mermaid who controls the sea?" It wasn't a joke, but Belle snorted and gave him a playful nudge.

"We're getting close," she said as they reentered the forest. The ground inclined steeply, and loose gravel made it impossible for the horse to keep his footing. Belle hummed in thought.

"We'll need to leave him here." She stopped and tied Philly to a tree.

Then she pulled out a bundle of rope. Nathaniel raised his brows at her. "What's that for? Are you going to tie me up too?"

This time, Belle made a hearty laugh, and it was music to Nathaniel's ears. He grinned, pleased that she thought he was funny, but equally pleased that tying him up wasn't part of her plan.

"We'll need this soon. Here, you need to drink." She handed him a sheepskin bag, and he took greedy gulps of water.

The only benefit to the crisp weather was that it kept the water cool. He handed it back to Belle, and their fingers brushed as she took it. The touch zinged Nathaniel's senses but he mentally shook himself to ignore it.

They scrambled up the hill in silence. The ground became so steep, they had to use the narrow tree trunks to steady themselves. Belle's cheeks flushed and she puffed hair out of her eyes as she surged forward. Nathaniel wondered if she was thinking about shifting.

Belle would have easily scaled the hill in wolf form, but they had agreed it was too dangerous after running into the wolf hunters.

"Almost there, I can see the top," she said, looking up. A weak beam of sunlight illuminated the shiny film of sweat above her upper lip. Nathaniel gritted his teeth as the ground moved beneath his feet. He daren't look back, though he didn't remember whether he was afraid of heights or not, the heart pounding in his chest told him that looking down wouldn't do him any good.

Finally, they made it to the top of the hill, and without hesitation, Belle tied one end of the rope to a thick tree trunk, then threw the rest over the edge. She tugged on it, testing the strength of the knot. Nathaniel joined her and peered down. The hill had brought them to the crest of a cliff, which was almost completely flat, with hardly any footings. A gust of salty air hit his face as he looked at the small beach at the bottom. In the water sat a cave on a tiny patch of land surrounded by rocks.

"Lexa was right. With those jagged boulders in the water, we'd never make it there by sea," Nathaniel said. If they had attempted the journey by boat, the raging waters would have thrown them on the sharp rocks, tearing the ship to pieces. Belle handed him the rope.

"Look," she said, gripping onto it and leaning over the edge.

Nathaniel wanted to hold his hand out protectively, but knew she was probably stronger than she looked and didn't need his help.

"If you tilt your head this way and look at the cave and all the rocks, it looks like an octopus."

Nathaniel couldn't help but smile. They were just about to abseil down a cliff with nothing but a rope to hold onto, and Belle acted like they were a couple of kids looking up at the clouds on a warm spring day.

"Are you sure you can do this with your wound?" he asked, worried.

Belle scoffed. "I can hardly feel it now. It's a lot better," she insisted. "Wolves heal fast, remember?"

Nathaniel wound the rope around his wrist and secured his grip. His stomach flipped several times as he went against all of his senses as he leaned back and grinned at Belle, who watched him with surprise.

"You remember how to abseil?"

Nathaniel winked at her. "Knowledge. Like I said... Fascinating, right?"

The cliff face was smooth against his boots, but it was much easier to keep his footing than on the hill. He and Belle climbed down in silence, and within minutes Nathaniel jumped to the sandy floor. He reached up for Belle, and she gripped his shoulders as he held her waist. When he lowered her down, they stood so close that her breath tickled his face.

"Thanks," she said before letting it go.

Nathaniel stepped back and dropped his hands. He then pointed at the cliff looming over them. "Going down was easy enough. But I imagine it'll be a different story when we have to climb back up."

"With any luck, you'll have your memories. Maybe you'll remember you like rock climbing in your spare time."

"Do I?" Nathaniel asked.

Belle chucked. "Well, let's just hope you don't remember that you never leave the laboratory because you hate adventure."

Nathaniel smirked. That sounded about right. "Although," he thought aloud, giving her a wry smile, "I would argue that, according to my research papers, I was on the brink of a scientific breakthrough. And that sounds like an adventure to me."

"Well then, *adventure man*," Belle said, resting her hands on her hips. "Lead the way."

They turned, and a narrow stone path rose from the water, leading to the mouth of the cave. Nathaniel swaggered forward, grinning ear to ear at Belle's words.

The stone path was just wide enough for Nathaniel to walk by placing one foot in front of the other. He instinctively held out his arms to balance and tried to ignore the water lapping at his boots. At the halfway point, a gust of sea air almost knocked him sideways. He shouted over his shoulder. "Are you all right?"

"I'm fine. Just keep moving!" Belle shouted back. The closer they got to the cave, the more treacherous the waters became. Almost like the sea knew they were venturing into forbidden territory.

The mouth of the cave loomed ahead,

and as they reached it, the entrance was much larger than it appeared on the beach. The sea waves crashed around them like a pack of roaring lions. Belle appeared undeterred as she patted herself down and picked up a torch hanging innocently on the wall of the cave entrance. "This will come in handy," she said.

Nathaniel looked around. They were surrounded by water and sandstone. "It would... if we could make fire."

Belle stuffed a hand in the pocket of her pants and pulled out a pack of matches. "Prepare to be amazed," she said. Then she struck the match, lit the torch, and marched inside.

That woman is full of surprises, Nathaniel thought, wondering what else she had up her sleeve. Then he set his jaw and followed Belle into the cave.

The sickly scent of seaweed consumed Nathaniel's senses as he and Belle walked deeper into the cave. Their footsteps echoed like horse hooves, and the anticipation of what was to come escalated with each passing minute.

The orange glow from the torchlight illuminated the glistening rock walls, and droplets fell like diamonds to the floor, smashing into a million water fragments before sinking into the rock bed.

The path descended until they reached what appeared to be a dead end.

"This can't be right," Belle said, touching the wall with a hand and looking around.

Nathaniel hummed in thought. Whoever made this cave did not want people to visit. If the treacherous waters and razor-sharp rocks surrounding the entrance were not enough to put off curious travelers, the supposed dead end surely would.

"What are the odds the mermaid sent us on a wild goose chase?" he asked.

The torchlight rippled over the wall as she shook her head. "No. There must be a hidden entrance somewhere," she said.

Nathaniel looked up just as the torchlight illuminated faint markings. "Wait," he said, grasping her wrist to stop her from moving away. The reflection of the flames danced in her wide eyes as she blinked up at him, sending a bolt of energy to his chest. He tore his gaze from her and ran his index finger across the grooves in the wall.

Belle seemed to follow his line of sight because she drew in a gasp and moved closer. "I've never seen markings like these before," she whispered.

"I have," Nathaniel blurted out, surprised by the fact. "It's written in ancient Greek."

Belle hummed. "I can't read it," she said with a huff. Judging by the irritation in her voice, Nathaniel knew she was frustrated at not knowing what to do next.

"Here... hold the torch up close," he said, his hand still holding her wrist. He lifted it higher and cleared his throat with authority.

"Are you familiar with the story of Orpheus and Eurydice?"

"A little... why?" Belle asked, her brows pinched. "What does it say?"

Nathaniel closed his eyes, drawing information from the darkness in his mind. Then, he studied the markings again.

"*Charm your way like Orpheus to Eurydice. That which was lost, will be returned to thee. But do not make his grave mistake. For if you look back, you will never escape."*

Nathaniel finished reading and looked at Belle, who stared at him like he had not spoken a common word.

"How did you..." she began, but then she shut her eyes with a low grunt. "Never mind. Charm your way... that must be a clue to find the opening. How did Orpheus charm his way to Eurydice?"

Nathaniel rubbed his chin. "When she died, he was so stricken by grief that he went to the underworld to bring her back."

Belle's eyes lit up with recognition. "And his singing charmed the ferryman who took him to Hades—"

"—who was so moved by his music that he allowed Eurydice to return to the land of the living," Nathaniel added, grinning at Belle.

"You have to sing!" they said in unison, pointing to the other.

"Who, me?" they said together. Then Belle broke into a light laugh.

Nathaniel scratched the back of his neck, then shifted his weight to his other foot.

"I can't sing," he admitted.

Belle bumped her hip against him playfully. "You don't *know* that, do you?"

Nathaniel shrugged. Belle had a point. For all he knew, he could have the voice of an angel—though he thought that was unlikely. But he didn't want his first attempt to be in a cave, standing less than two feet from Belle.

"Would you do the honors?" he asked, lifting his brows. "Besides, I know for a fact you have a voice more beautiful than a mermaid."

Belle's cheeks reddened and she stepped back a little, as if the words struck her with an invisible force. "I don't know what to sing," she said, turning back to the wall.

"How about the flower song?"

Belle looked at him with a smirk. "The flower song?" she repeated, arching a brow.

Nathaniel shrugged again. "You know, the one you sang back at your cabin."

They looked at each other in a silent standoff, and a creeping smile took over Belle's worried face. Then she cleared her throat.

"Alright, hold this." She handed Nathaniel the torch and wiggled on the spot with a shuddering breath.

"Do you always do that before you sing?" Nathaniel asked, humored.

Belle shot him a look and puffed out her cheeks. "I do when I'm trying to charm a wall," she said in a breathy voice.

Nathaniel found her hand and gave it a reassuring squeeze. "Hey, I have every faith in you."

Belle's eyes softened. She turned to face the wall again. Then she opened her mouth and began to sing.

As the melody was carried through the cave, every muscle in his body relaxed, and he slipped into a state of bliss. He could have stood in the mouth of an active volcano, and he was certain he'd remain perfectly calm. Belle's voice was tender and soft. Like a gentle purr and a succession of sweet kisses to his eardrums.

But then the beautiful sound was taken over by the jarring of rock scraping against rock. Nathaniel opened his eyes—not realizing he had closed them—and watched the wall split in two, creating an opening just big enough for a person to walk through.

Belle and Nathaniel looked at each other. "You did it!" Nathaniel cheered.

Belle took the torch off him with a smug smile. "You sound surprised," she shot back and marched forward, her hips swaying.

After a few moments, Nathaniel caught himself watching her, entranced by the way her body moved, and picked up a brisk walk to catch up.

As soon as he walked through the opening, the ground rumbled, and Nathaniel didn't need to look to know the wall had closed behind them.

"Didn't it say something about not looking back?" Belle said, her voice echoing.

"Right," Nathaniel replied as they walked. "You'll just have to resist the temptation to catch another glimpse of my devilishly handsome face."

Belle's shoulders shook. "You really are your brother's twin," she teased.

But before Nathaniel could reply, he lost his footing and slipped, dropping the torch and crashing to the smooth ground. He slid forward as the path turned into a large swirling slide.

The two of them scrambled to catch the walls or grip onto a passing rock. They kept sliding with more speed until they rounded a bend, and the ground suddenly disappeared.

They dropped on a patch of sand, and Belle screeched as they came to an abrupt stop. The force knocked her forward, and she rolled over the edge of a cliff. Quick as a flash, Nathaniel grabbed her.

"Hold on, I've got you," he said through gritted teeth as he pulled her up. Belle helped by grabbing onto the rocky cliff and pulling.

Once safely back at the top, Nathaniel scanned her from head to toe. "Are you okay?" he asked, breathless.

"I think so." Belle pushed herself to her feet and patted down her cloak. "Quick reflex."

"Thanks."

A flash of electric blue light caught Nathaniel's attention and they peeked over the edge to see a glittering pool of untouched water.

"That must be it," Belle said. "Are we supposed to jump? Looks like a huge drop."

Nathaniel chewed his lip in thought as he

looked for a way down. He spotted an iron cage on the side of the cliff. For a flash, he remembered the iron mask and tugged on his shirt collar, the memory constricting his throat.

"Look," he said, pointing to it. "There's a pulley system. I think we can use this to get down."

Belle frowned so deeply; a line formed between her brows. "It's only big enough for one of us. I'll have to stay up here and lower you down," she said, but the look on her face told Nathaniel she didn't like the plan one bit.

He stepped into the cage and turned back to face her. "I'll be right back."

Belle nodded and gripped the handle and wound the winch. Nathaniel lowered until Belle was out of sight, then he shuffled around to get a better look at where he was going.

Blue ethereal light lit up the water, and a saccharine perfume scent grew stronger as he reached the bottom. With a clank, the iron met the rock bed and Nathaniel stepped out. He craned his neck to see Belle, looking the size of a cat and waved up at her.

He looked at the winch by the wall and

was about to grab the handle when a skin-crawling squeal stopped him in his tracks.

"Well, well, well... who do we have here?"

The bellowing voice reverberated through the entire cave, making the ground quake beneath Nathaniel's boots. Blue light flashed like lightning with a crackle, and a tremendous splash covered Nathaniel from head to toe in ice cold water.

Blinking the moisture out of his eyes, Nathaniel panted and staggered forward until he reached the edge of the pool. Then his gaze stopped on something his brain struggled to process.

A dark purple tentacle slid across the slimy rock floor and disappeared back into the water again.

A deep guttural groan flooded the air, growing louder as a large woman emerged from the water. A crown of white hair lay in soft waves, rippling and hanging over the woman's broad shoulders. Her skin looked iridescent as it reflected the water, and two inky eyes rested on Nathaniel.

"You!" the woman roared as she lifted

herself up, her ample bosom covered in purple scales.

Nathaniel gulped and took a step back as his gaze lowered. Where the woman's belly button should have been was a scaly torso, splitting into eight long tentacles. One of which slipped out of the water and slid closer to Nathaniel's boots.

The half-woman, half-octopus gave Nathaniel no time to process his thoughts and thrust a tentacle at him, but not before he ducked out of the way.

With a frustrated screech, another tentacle came flying in his direction, narrowly missing his face. Nathaniel rolled and jumped up, his heart pounding. He looked from left to right, searching for something he could use as a weapon. But there wasn't so much as a rock on the smooth rock bed, and the water lapped at his heels, rising as the monster woman thrashed.

"I mean you no harm!" he said as loud as he could while keeping his voice steady. He strained his ears, trying to listen out for Belle, who stood several hundred feet above. But he daren't look up and direct the monster's attention toward her.

So long as he kept her focus on him, Belle was safe.

"No harm?" The female creature threw her head back and chuckled so deeply, the vibrations ran through Nathaniel's body, tangling his insides. "What a relief." She placed the back of her hand against her brow, her voice dripping with sarcasm. "I thought you had come to cut off my head."

Nathaniel stood tall and set his hands on his hips, studying the woman carefully. She possessed a sense of humor, so he wondered how she might respond to flattery.

"I have come from a faraway land just to see you," he began. "Why would I want to cut off that beautiful head of yours?"

"Beautiful, you say?" she replied, her composure softening. Her voice turned silky as she edged closer to him, her tentacles slipping back into the water. "You're quite the charmer. And what am I to call you?"

"My name is Nathaniel, and you are...?" Nathaniel tapped his legs, looking around in the vain hope her name might be on the walls.

CHAPTER 8

"Neri," the woman said. "You may call me Neri."

Nathaniel's shoulders relaxed. "That's a Greek name, correct?"

Neri chuckled warmly and settled lower into the water. "Well, well, well. This is a rare meeting. It's not every day I get human visitors. Usually, it's just desperate mermaids looking for solutions to their problems. Is that why you're here?"

"I've heard that your water is quite special," Nathaniel said, trying to hide the anticipation in his voice. "Would you tell me about it?"

"Well, seeing as you asked so nicely…" Neri rubbed her chin with a rumbling hum. "My water has the purest minerals in all the realms. No one knows how, but whoever drinks this water shall be cured of any ailment."

"Would memory loss be considered an ailment?" Nathaniel asked, giving her a casual smile. Neri's eyes narrowed on him.

"Ah, so you want a taste of my water too, I see." She didn't sound angry, much to Nathaniel's surprise. Instead, her glittering eyes looked him up and down and a wicked grin crossed her painted lips. "Perhaps we could make an exchange?"

Nathaniel gave her a quizzical look. "What kind of exchange?"

Without another word, Neri lifted one of her tentacles from the water and stretched it out in front of Nathaniel as if it were an open hand. An empty vial came into view, and she smiled. "A drop of your blood for a drink of my water."

Nathaniel didn't like the deal, but the desperation for his memories was stronger. He reached down and picked up a broken shell from the edge of the water. He made a small cut on his palm, feeling the burn spread over his hand. As soon as blood began seeping out, he balled his hand into a fist and held it over the glass, watching as his blood dropped into the vial.

Once he pulled his hand away, he threw the shell aside then watched as she sealed the vial and hid it back underneath the water. He gave the octopus woman a serious look. But before he could remind her that it was her turn to keep her end of the deal, she lifted a bowl-shaped shell from the water with two tentacles and offered it to Nathaniel. He took it, eyeing the sparkling water inside.

"What are you waiting for?" she asked, the wicked grin still on her face. "Drink."

Nathaniel took one last look at her, then at the shell in his hands. The water swirled around, and the scientific side of Nathaniel's brain wondered how this could possibly return his memories. But he pushed away his skepticism and gulped the water down before he could change his mind.

"Well? How do you feel?" Neri asked. Nathaniel wiped his mouth with the back of his hand and looked up at her as he set the shell on the ground.

"The same," he said with a shrug. He wasn't sure what he expected. He thought his head might spin. Or he'd sense a rush of adrenaline. But instead, he felt nothing. Not even a twinge in his stomach.

"Give it time. I may be many things, but a liar I am not," Neri assured him. Then she waved a hand dramatically, and the sound of rock scraping against rock filled the air. "Now, go on your way. We are done here."

And just like that, Neri dipped below the surface of the water, and a mass of bubbles scattered across the top. Nathaniel returned to the cage and shouted up to Belle. After she pulled him up to rejoin her, an opening appeared in the wall.

Nathaniel wasted no time in getting out of there with Belle. They stepped out onto a narrow pathway that hugged the side of the cave. The once thrashing seas sat still, and the setting sunshine scattered across the smooth surface like glitter.

"How was it?" Belle asked, looking at Nathaniel with curious eyes.

Nathaniel narrowed his eyes, wondering how best to describe it. "Strange."

"Why do you say that?" Belled asked. "Was it because she asked for a drop of your blood?"

Nathaniel gave Belle a surprised look.

She shrugged. "I could hear from miles away. It's a wolf thing. But I couldn't see her. What was she like? Was she a mermaid?"

"Not exactly," Nathaniel said. "She was... half-octopus. Which I guess explains the cave and rock layout you noticed before."

Belle's cheeks flushed as her mouth formed a perfect O. "I would've liked seeing that."

They crossed the path. This time, the waters had calmed, making the trip much easier.

"Well, did it work?" Belle asked as they returned to the beach. "Can you remember anything?"

Nathaniel shook his head, a sense of disappointment sinking in his chest. "It's getting dark. We should hurry back to the horse," he murmured as they reached the cliff. He tugged on the rope, checking that it was still secure, then passed it to Belle. She grinned at him, her cheeks flushed.

"I can't believe we did it," she said, triumphant.

"Well, don't get too excited. Nothing's happened yet," Nathaniel said, trying to ignore the jitters in his stomach.

"I know, but I heard what Neri said, you have to give it time."

They climbed in silence, huffing as they focused on scaling the smooth rock. Once Nathaniel joined Belle at the top, only the crest of the sun appeared above the ocean.

As they slid down the rocky hill, a sharp pain shot through Nathaniel's temple like someone had stabbed him with a knife. But the pain disappeared as quickly as it came. He rubbed his head with a frown as he followed Belle to where they tied her horse.

"Belle..."

When Belle swiveled, her eyes grew wide. Nathaniel's frown deepened at her concern. He wanted to ask what was wrong, but his mouth refused to obey his thoughts. Then the world slanted, and the ground shifted like somebody pulled the rug from beneath his feet.

"Nathaniel!" Belle's scream sounded far away, like a distant siren, as Nathaniel sank to his knees and his vision darkened. Then he slumped forward, and everything grew black.

CHAPTER 9

Belle

Belle wasn't one to panic often, but when Nathaniel passed out after drinking whatever water he ingested, she couldn't think straight. Her first instinct was to shift into her wolf form and carry him as fast as possible to the only healer she knew she could trust.

Marian.

Before long, Belle found herself shrinking in her chair as Marian sat on the edge of her bed, staring at her brother lying unconscious with a wet rag resting on his forehead. As much as she wanted to, Belle couldn't bring herself to approach. She had no idea what was going through her friend's mind, but she wouldn't blame her for being upset. Belle had omitted the truth, and that was just as bad as a lie. A million apologies rushed through Belle's mind, but she didn't dare say a word.

Nathaniel was burning up with fever, and despite the cream Marian had been rubbing on his chest for hours, he still hadn't woken up.

There was so much Belle wanted to say, but she lost all courage to speak. She should've told Marian about Nathaniel. Even with all the reasons she had not to, none of it mattered when she saw her friend's eyes fill with tears.

"What happened to him?" Marian asked, her voice soft in the candlelit room.

Belle rose to her feet and took a hesitant step forward. She had already told Marian about the Reditus Cave, and the water that was supposed to have given him his memories back. But if she wanted to hear it all again, it was the least Belle could do.

Belle cleared her throat, then told Marian

everything once more. Except for when he went down the cage. Belle couldn't see exactly what had happened down below, she could only hear the conversation they had, but he seemed fine when he came back up.

"Did you bring a sample of that water with you?" Marian asked, turning to look at Belle for the first time since they'd arrived.

Belle took another step forward. "I'm so sorry, Marian—"

"Just answer the question, Belle."

"I already told you, I didn't get a sample," Belle replied. "And I'm sorry. I am so deeply sorry I kept this from you."

Marian rose to her feet with a scowl. "You should have told me."

"I know." Belle frowned. "And believe me, I wanted to. I even asked him. But he was afraid it would be too overwhelming." And she was also afraid that Marian had helped lock him up, but Belle kept that to herself. Judging by how relieved she was to see him, it was clear that Marian had nothing to do with that wicked scheme.

"Afraid it would be too overwhelming?" Marian repeated in disbelief. "I'm his sister."

"Who he didn't remember," Belle reasoned. "Please, Marian. Don't take this personally. I'm sure that if he remembered you, he wouldn't have hesitated. And neither would I. Please, forgive me."

Marian took a blood sample from her brother's arm, then walked across the room to a pot on the stove. "I just want to know what was in that blazing water."

"Mer?" Nathaniel's voice was soft, but it seemed to have landed in Marian's ears like a thunderstorm. She swung around with a gasp.

"Nate!"

Leaving the small vial of blood on the counter, she ran toward the bed and into her brother's arms. He enveloped her in a tight embrace as he sat up.

"You remember your sister?" Belle asked, surprised.

Nathaniel lifted his eyes to look at her. It took a few seconds to process the meaning of her words, but then a smile spread across his face. "I do." He pulled back to take a better look at his sister. Seeing her so close made his smile even wider. "My memories are coming back!"

The wooden floor creaked when he jumped to his feet in excitement, and Belle felt a strong pull toward him. But she stood her ground. As much as she worried that he could've been overdoing it with the swift movements, Belle feared that if she reached for him and laid him back down, his sister would get the wrong idea.

"Did you not hear me?" Nathaniel rushed toward Belle with a grin. "It worked!"

Before she could stop him, he picked her up off the floor and spun her around. The air in the room buzzed with energy and every atom of Belle's body trembled at being in Nathaniel's strong arms. When her feet found the floor again, she placed her hands on his chest with the intent to push him away, but his smile was so hypnotic, she couldn't bring herself to.

"Thank you," he said softly, his warm breath tickling her face.

Belle opened her mouth to respond, but his mouth was so close to hers, she lost all train of thought. And the fact that her body was pressed up to his chest so tightly she could feel his pectorals tense didn't help to cool her down.

The sound of Marian clearing her throat across the room jolted the both of them to pull away. Belle's cheeks grew hot, and she lowered her eyes.

"Did you really lose your memory?" Marian asked her brother. "What happened?"

Nathaniel turned to face his sister. "Prince John," he said. "He kept me locked in a dungeon."

"But Emmett said you were sick," Marian said, sitting on the edge of her bed. "That's why he sent you away."

"I was never sick, Mer." An angry crease formed between Nathaniel's brows as he stared at the floor. Belle imagined the memories were returning and playing out in his mind. "He just wanted me out of his way so he could become king."

"Nate, that's not what happened—"

"I remember, Mer. Prince John came to meet with me. He wanted an alliance with our kingdom, as well as your hand in marriage, but I refused him," Nathaniel explained. "I refused everything. Especially *you*. I would never have subjected you to a loveless marriage, and I told him that."

Marian stood and made her way to him. "Why don't you sit down?" She tried to take his arm, but he moved it away.

"Don't you see?" He looked up at her, a sense of urgency in his eyes. "Emmett handed me over to be locked away like a prisoner so he could take my throne and accept the alliance with Prince John. It makes perfect sense."

Belle wouldn't put it past Emmett having done such a horrendous thing, but she didn't dare say a word. This was a family issue, and it wasn't her place.

Marian's frown deepened, and she picked on a loose thread on her dress. "You're making an assumption—"

"Did he or did he not accept an alliance with Prince John?" Nathaniel asked, towering over his sister.

She scowled at the floor. "He did, but—"

"And did he or did he not hand you over to marry that despicable Prince?" Nathaniel gave his sister a pointed look. She didn't have to answer. He knew about the wedding. Will and Red had filled him in on the whole story. And Belle confirmed everything. There was no denying it.

"That was different," Marian said, her expression softening.

"No, it wasn't," Nathaniel pressed. "He locked me in a prison just as he was going to lock you in a loveless marriage. He betrayed us both, and you know it."

"I still don't think—"

Nathaniel threw his arms in the air with a frustrated grunt. "This was all his fault. Because of his greed, you have no idea what I've done. What I've created!"

That caught Marian's attention because she lifted her eyes filled with tears and stared at her brother for a long moment. Belle could tell Marian wanted to say something, but Nathaniel was still talking.

"And what about my memories?" he continued. "How convenient for me to forget that *I'm* the rightful heir to the throne."

"Nathaniel, stop." Tears slid down Marian's cheeks as she raised a hand.

"Why are you defending him?" Nathaniel gave his sister a look of disbelief. But then something changed in his eyes. It was as if a new memory had surfaced in his mind, and he cocked his head. "You knew." The air shifted and grew heavy as he gave her a piercing look. Belle pushed her cuticles as she hovered by the door, wondering whether to give them privacy, but this was news to her too, and the lure to know more kept her rooted on the spot.

When Marian didn't respond, Nathaniel stepped away from her. "You knew he handed me over." His voice barely made it out. "You were in on it with him." He lowered to a chair by the window, his shoulders dropping.

"Emmett told me you were sick," Marian confessed. "Prince John offered to help you in exchange for an alliance. In exchange for my hand in marriage. *That* was the reason he handed you over. That's what I was told."

Nathaniel shook his head in disbelief.

"Nate, please…" Marian tried reaching for him again, but he stood and moved away from her. "I was only told about it after you were gone. I would never have allowed them to take you had they done it in front of me. You know that."

Nathaniel rubbed his tired eyes, then ran a

hand over the length of his hair. "I need to clear my head."

As much as Belle wanted to follow after him when he disappeared into the other room, she fought back the urge and stood still.

But then Marian turned to her with tears sliding down her face, and Belle rushed to her friend's side.

"I thought he was sick," Marian said with a sniff. "I can't believe Emmett lied to me."

Belle guided her friend to the nearest seat by the crackling fire, then sat next to her. Despite the warmth, goosebumps covered her arms and she shuddered, the night's events giving her a chill.

"Marian, listen to me..." She glanced over her shoulder to make sure Nathaniel wasn't listening, then turned to meet Marian's eyes. "Your brother *is* sick. Of course, I don't think Prince John had any intention of helping him, but Nathaniel's been having blackouts and hallucinations. And I'm not sure that getting his memories back will make that go away."

Before Belle could say another word, Marian jumped to her feet and wiped her wet face. "There's only one way to find out," she said, rushing across the room and grabbing her brother's blood vial from the counter before hurrying toward the pot of boiling water.

Belle followed her to the stove and watched as Marian rummaged through the cupboard. Glasses clinked, and she muttered under her breath until she pulled out a jar of dried leaves. Without hesitation, she opened it and emptied the leaves out. They dropped into the boiling water with a hiss. Once the plant began to change color, Marian opened the vial and let a drop of blood fall into the pot. The two of them peered over the boiling pot with bated breath.

When nothing happened, Belle looked at Marian. "Now what?"

Marian sighed. "Now, we wait." She pulled back and crossed her arms. When neither of them spoke for several seconds, Marian looked at Belle with a frown.

"What?" Belle asked, curious as to the source of her friend's unease.

"I don't think Emmett sent Nathaniel away because he wanted the throne," Marian said wryly.

"Can you think of any other reason?" Belle asked.

"My parents..." Marian said, wrapping her arms around herself as if trying to physically keep it together. "They were killed by a wolf."

Belle's eyes widened. "What?"

Marian shook her head. "I wasn't there, but Emmett was. And it wasn't just any wolf." She leaned in, and her eyes shot to the door, then she lowered her voice as if to utter a confession. "It was a wolf that Nathaniel brought into the palace and nursed back to health."

Belle's mouth dropped open. "That would certainly explain Emmett's hatred for the wolves," she muttered under her breath.

Marian nodded. "And I wouldn't be surprised if he blamed Nathaniel for our parents' death."

"You think?" Belle whispered, not bothering to tell Marian about the iron mask. Maybe that was Prince John's doing and not Emmett's. "Does Nathaniel know? About your parents?"

"If his memories really are coming

back…" Marian glanced toward the bedroom briefly, then back at Belle. "Then it's only a matter of time before he does."

A faint glow came from the pot on the stove, and Belle followed Marian's gaze toward the boiling water.

Marian gasped, sending a wave of chills down Belle's spine.

"What?" Belle asked, peering into the water. The glow grew brighter by the second, but then it turned blue. "Marian, what's wrong?"

"The blood sample," she replied. "It's the same as the one you brought to me before."

"Oh. Right." Belle winced with guilt. "I'm sorry I didn't tell you—"

"No, Belle. That's not the problem." Marian pointed to the glowing water again. "This blood sample has traces of…"

When Marian didn't finish, Belle wondered if she was going to mention *mermaid scales*. That was what Marian had found on Nathaniel's blood last time. But when Marian's color drained from her face, Belle could tell there was more to it.

"Traces of what?" Belle pressed.

Marian turned to meet Belle's eyes. "Wolf DNA."

Before Belle could respond, a snarl came from across the room. The hairs on the back of her neck stood on end as she turned around slowly, only to find a pair of crimson eyes scowling back at her.

Marian gasped, dropping a glass. It hit the floor with a tremendous smash, but no one paid any attention. All eyes were on the huge wolf with shaggy black hair standing in the doorway.

Another snarl ripped from the beast as he stepped onto the light. Belle moved slowly to stand in front of Marian. When he growled again, Belle lifted a hand to keep him at bay. "Nathaniel…"

Nathaniel is not here. When his voice entered her mind, Belle gasped. It was Nathaniel's voice. It was still muffed, which was why it was hard for her to recognize, but hearing him at that moment, there was no mistaking it. Marian grabbed Belle's arm and squeezed. She touched Marian's hand without looking away from the beast's red eyes.

"I know you're in there," Belle said,

keeping her voice soft and unthreatening. "Remember what Lexa said, Prince John is controlling you. You can break free, Nathaniel. Just come back to us."

The beast stood on his hind legs and puffed out his chest, his breath smothering them in hot vapor. But before he could respond, the window shattered, and an arrow snapped in two as it collided with his chest.

Once the shattered arrow fell to the floor, the beast turned toward the broken window and howled. Marian stepped back while Belle threw her hands in the air. "Nathaniel, look at me!"

His crimson eyes locked on hers with a scowl. He growled in frustration, and before she could say anything else, he bolted out the door.

"Nathaniel, wait!"

Another arrow hit the beast's back, but also shattered to the floor after colliding with his impenetrable skin. Belle's mind scrambled to make sense of what was happening. When he disappeared into the distance, a loud thud of heavy boots came from the window.

Belle swung around to catch the hunter

who had attacked the beast. A dark green hood covered his face, and just a tuft of blonde hair was visible.

"Who're you?" Belle asked.

He grunted at seeing that the beast had escaped, then pulled the hood from his head.

"Robin?" Marian blinked several times, perhaps to make sure her eyes weren't playing tricks on her. "Where on earth have you been?"

He turned to face her with an emotionless expression. "I was hired to hunt down that beast."

"A *beast*?" Marian stared at him as if he'd slapped her. "You left to hunt down a *beast*? Everyone is worried sick about you. Your cousin was starting to think you were dead! How insensitive—"

Belle put a hand on Marian's shoulder, knowing her friend was mostly hysterical about having just witnessed her brother shift into a monster before her eyes. But also because there was something strange in Robin's expression and the way he was looking at Marian. It was cold.

"Robin…" Belle said softly, then waited

for him to look at her. "Do you remember who we are?"

A small smile tugged at the corner of his lips. "You're Belle, and you…" He turned to Marian with a smug look. "Are the stubborn princess who never needed saving. All the wasted effort."

Marian seemed taken aback by his tone. It was clear he'd never spoken to her like that. Or even looked at her in such a careless manner.

"What happened to you?" Belle asked. "Who took you?"

"The Snow Queen freed me from a life of unwanted responsibility," he replied with a relieved tone. As if the thought of no longer being a leader made him feel lighter than air. "And of course…" His eyes flickered toward Marian. "Needless heartache. Now, if you'll excuse me. I have a beast to catch."

As Robin walked past them, Marian took a knife from the kitchen and cut his arm.

He swung around with a scowl. "What was that for?" he hissed, covering the cut with his hand. The cut was fairly small but just enough to sting.

"If you ever barge into my house like that again," she said, narrowing her eyes at him. "The next cut will be at your throat."

The corner of Robin's lips lifted. "I've underestimated you, Princess." He bowed his head politely. "My apologies for the intrusion."

Marian lowered the knife with a frown. "This isn't you, Robin."

His expression turned serious again. "I guess a man knows when to stop begging." And with that, he turned around and walked out the door. Marian leaned back against the counter, staring at where Robin had been. Belle wasn't sure what was going through her friend's mind, but she was flushed and sad, and still holding the bloody knife.

"Are you all right?" Belle stared at her friend with concern. "I mean, it's not like you to cut someone."

Marian was silent for a few seconds, then shook her head as if returning from her thoughts. "I know, I just needed a sample of his blood. I need to find out what The Snow Queen did to him." Belle had never seen

CHAPTER 9

Marian genuinely concerned about Robin before.

"Well, let me know what you find. I need to go," Belle said, reaching for her bag on the counter. "I need to find your brother before Robin does."

Marian nodded. "Just be careful," she said. "I've heard that Emmett sent out word to all hunters to kill every wolf in the forest."

Belle tightened the strap of her satchel around her shoulder, then put an encouraging hand on her friend's shoulder. "I will find him. I promise."

Belle ran out and found Philly grazing on a patch of grass in the street. Grateful to see that he had followed her, Belle mounted the horse. She would much rather have shifted into wolf form, but Marian was right. The forest was teeming with hunters, and Belle had already fallen into one of their traps. She couldn't risk getting injured again. Or worse... killed.

She needed to find Nathaniel. And the cure—now more than ever.

*A*s Belle arrived at a neighboring village, a fallen carriage blocked her path. It lay on its side, the back wheel spinning, and a trail of disaster cut through the square. Trampled flowers lay strewn all over the ground and the ashen-white faces of the villagers huddled in the street told her the beast had been there.

"Belle!" a woman's voice called out from behind, and Belle looked over her shoulder. A young woman ran toward Belle. Her gray cotton dress billowed out behind her, and she touched her blonde hair, perhaps to check it was still pulled up in a bun. Belle's heart ached at the tears welling in the young woman's crystal-blue eyes. Though she tried to mask her fear with a fixed smile.

"Ella!" Belle dismounted her horse and pulled the woman in a tight hug. "It's been years! Last time I saw you must have been while my father was working for your father," Belle said as they broke apart, but she squeezed Ella's slender hands, not ready to let go just yet. They were good friends growing up, spending many summer days rolling down the hills and picking flowers in the meadows. "What are you doing here?"

Ella's beaming expression turned sad, and the tears in her eyes wobbled, threatening to fall. "My father passed away," she said. "I live with my stepmother now. She sold my father's manor and bought Stanley Manor up the hill. I come to this village to pick up hay for the stables."

"Oh, Ella. I am so sorry about your father." Belle put a hand on her friend's shoulder. "When did this happen?"

Ella shrugged, averting her gaze. "He was sick. Your father was so sweet during that time. It broke my heart to let him go."

"Let him go?" Belle echoed.

"When my stepmother moved us here, everyone lost their jobs," Ella said. "Anyway, I don't want to bore you with all the details. What are you doing here?"

Belle opened her mouth to speak, but her thoughts were still on her father, and how she had no idea that he lost his job. It was a stark reminder of just how long Belle had stayed away from him, and she wondered how much she had missed.

"Belle?"

"Right." Belle shook off her concern for her father. "I came from visiting my brother at Sherwood Forest. I was just stopping to give Philly some water." It wasn't entirely a lie, but it wasn't like she could tell her the truth. She looked around at the damage. "What happened here?"

"The beast," Ella replied, her voice lowering. "He's come around before, but never during the day."

"Did he hurt anyone?"

"Not that I know of, but everyone is pretty shaken up. My own heartbeat is only just starting to slow down. But I heard it took something from the metalsmith."

"The metalsmith?" Belle asked, searching her friend's eyes. "Do you know what it was?"

"A genie bracelet," Ella said. The only genie bracelet Belle had ever heard of was the one Aria was looking for. The one that inhibited her powers. But why would Prince John want the bracelet? Could he be planning to turn against Aria?

Back at Marian's house, the beast said Nathaniel wasn't there. Which would explain the blackouts. Whenever he shifted, he was mind-controlled by Prince John.

"I have to go," Belle said, giving Ella a quick hug. "It was so good to see you."

Ella said something back, but Belle's mind was flipping through a million things. She mounted her horse and sniffed the air. She caught the floral scent of her soap, which Nathaniel had used.

He was back in human form.

How did Belle not notice Nathaniel was a wolf? She had been so focused on getting his memories back so she could finally get the wolf cure that it had left her blindsided.

Belle caught Nathaniel's scent moments before she spotted him lying facing down on the ground by a tree. She jumped off Philly and ran to Nathaniel's side. She quickly removed her cloak and covered him with it. He groaned as he rolled to his side. She looked around for the genie bracelet he had taken, but it was nowhere in sight.

"Nathaniel," she spoke softly, wiping his hair from his clammy forehead. "Say something."

"Belle?" He squinted as he looked up at her. "What happened?" As he looked down at himself, a flicker of panic rose in his eyes. "I'm naked. Where are we, and where's my sister?"

"You had another blackout," Belle explained, forcing an unconcerned smile. She then grabbed a bag from the saddle and handed it to him. "But I see you still remember your sister. That's good." She forced another smile.

Nathaniel pulled out a set of clothes, and his tense shoulders relaxed. "I do." He offered a tired smile. "And my brother, too."

Belle averted her eyes as he wasted no time to dress himself. When he rose to his feet, Belle helped him up. "What about... your parents?" she asked. "Do you remember them?"

Nathaniel didn't respond as he tied the collar of his white, oversized shirt. Belle's heart raced with curiosity, wondering if he knew the truth about what had happened to his parents.

"I don't remember," he said, sadness

evident in his tone. He turned to meet Belle's eyes. "Why don't I remember them?"

"Your memories are coming back slowly," Belle explained. "I'm sure that in time you'll remember everything."

Belle's stomach churned. Time was her worst enemy at the moment. She needed to find the cure before he remembered what happened to his parents. Before he discovered that their death was his fault. But most importantly, before he realized he didn't just create the beast. He *was* the beast.

"Come on." Belle hooked her arm under his. "Let's go home."

"Wait…" He stopped her. "I remember something else."

Chills shot down Belle's spine as she gulped. "What is it?"

"The cure," he said with a smile spreading across his face. "I remember how to make it."

Belle's eyes widened in disbelief. "You remember the ingredients?"

He nodded. "Every single one of them."

Belle's heart lifted in her chest. "Nathaniel, that's amazing!"

"No." He cupped her face in his strong hands. "*You're* amazing, Belle."

Her cheeks grew hot against his palms, but she couldn't look away from his blue eyes. They were so captivating.

"Making the cure for you is the least I can do for all you've done for me," he said, peering into her eyes. "I just need to make sure that's really what you want."

"It is," she said quickly. But she was no longer thinking of herself. As much as she wanted to get rid of the wolf inside her, the desperate need to get rid of the beast controlling Nathaniel was stronger.

"All right, then," Nathaniel's smile grew wider. "Let's go make that cure."

Belle knew the best chance of finding all of the ingredients on Nathaniel's list was in Luton, a town known for its huge market. All kinds of rare and curious artifacts were sold by merchants from all over the kingdom. Belle and Nathaniel shouldered their way through the crowded streets. Hundreds of tents squeezed into the square, and the smell of spices and wild game filled the air as they walked.

Belle's horse whinnied and tossed his head, the strength almost pulling Belle's arm out of her socket as she tried to restrain him. "Come on, boy, let's take you somewhere quiet." She shushed Philly and smoothed his mane, then led him to a nearby post with a line of horses drinking from the same trough.

After tying the reins to keep him secure, Belle found Nathaniel entering the busy marketplace.

Belle rubbed her eyes as she followed after him. She had barely slept the night before. The fear of Nathaniel shifting into a beast and running wild through the forest kept her up most of the night. Also, the guilt of not telling him what she knew weighed heavily on her conscience. He had the right to know, but he already felt so guilty thinking he created the monster. How awful would he feel to find out he *was* the monster?

When Belle finally caught up with Nathaniel, he had his arms full. "I've found all

I need, except one ingredient. But no one seems to have it."

An elderly man stepped in their path, his gray eyes lingered on the plants and vials in Nathaniel's arms before he grinned at him. "It looks like you're in the market for some rare herbs. Maybe I can be of assistance?"

He led them into his small tent and away from the bustling crowd. Belle resisted the urge to wince at the stifling scent of herbs and burning incense. A table full of all manner of strange objects took her attention.

"Now, what are you looking for?" the merchant asked, taking his spot behind the table.

"I'm looking for red rose essence, it's an oil distilled from the—"

"A wild red rose. Of course..." the man said, tapping a wrinkled finger to his thin lips. "But alas, you shall struggle to find it within fifty miles of here."

"Why do you say that?" Belle asked.

The old man looked at her and leaned in close. "There are whispers all through the town of a terrible beast that is on the loose and has been going from village to village."

Belle's stomach twinged with guilt as she glanced at Nathaniel. "But what has that got to do with—"

"The wild red rose essence is believed to be poisonous to wolves. Just one drop is enough to trigger an allergic reaction, but don't play coy, you knew this, of course," the old man said, keeping his voice low.

Belle bit her lip as her mind worked overtime to come up with a lie. "Right. We were hoping to use it... for protection."

The old man surveyed her closely with a deep hum before he leaned back, and Belle could breathe again. "If it is protection you're seeking, I may have something else you could use." The merchant pulled out a cloth from his satchel and lifted it toward Nathaniel. He unwrapped the cloth, unveiling a dandelion in a small glass case.

"A flower?"

The merchant smiled. "Not just any flower," he clarified. "It's a honey seedhead dandelion."

Belle leaned forward to examine it. "What does it do?"

"That's not going to help us," Nathaniel

said, pulling back.

"Maybe it could," Belle replied, keeping her eyes on the flower. "How does it work?"

Belle reached out to hold it, but the merchant pulled it away. "You cannot touch it unless you're ready to make your wish," he warned.

"It grants wishes?" Belle asked, intrigued.

"It grants you *one* wish, but at great cost," Nathaniel cut in, not even bothering to look at the flower. He turned to the merchant. "We're not going to need it. Thank you."

Nathaniel walked away and headed toward another tent. Belle was about to follow after him but found herself hesitating. The merchant must've noticed because he kept the dandelion raised in front of her.

"How *exactly* does it work?" she whispered.

The merchant smiled. "It's simple... you make a wish then blow on it to the wind."

Belle bit her bottom lip. "What's the catch?"

The merchant shrugged. "Every medicine has side effects. The real question is... how much are you willing to sacrifice for your wish?"

Belle glanced at Nathaniel across the market. What if the cure didn't work? After all, his memories weren't quite fully back. She needed a backup plan. "I'll take it," she said quickly. He wrapped the dandelion seedhead back in the cloth, then handed it to her after she gave him the money. She shoved the glass casing into her satchel and ran to catch up with Nathaniel.

He met her halfway, then let out a frustrated sigh. "The old man was right, everyone is sold out." He scratched the back of his neck. "We can try another marketplace."

Belle shook her head. "We can't waste any more time. I know where we can find a wild red rose."

"Where?" Nathaniel asked, his brows shooting up.

Belle knew there was one person who collected rare herbs and oils. And he happened to also be the one person she had avoided for all this time. But she had no other choice.

Belle inhaled sharply. "It's time to pay my father a visit."

CHAPTER 10

Nathaniel

Nathaniel's mind raced, thoughts running into thoughts at a never-ending speed as old memories flooded him. Whatever was in the water Neri had given him, it was working.

Where there was once darkness in his mind, now there were faces. His twin brother, Emmett, who he used to poke fun at when they were kids for being three minutes younger than him. Then there was their little sister, Marian. With thick, wiry hair and blue eyes, she was the carbon copy of their mother. His mother's face was a new memory. His father, on the other hand, was still hazy in his mind. Nathaniel knew they had died, but he couldn't remember how.

A tangle of jumbled emotions swirled inside of him at the thought of his mother. A distinct memory swept across his mind of her sitting by his bed, brushing damp hair from his forehead and singing a lullaby to him.

Nathaniel swallowed and tried to ignore the prickling sensation in his eyes, and instead, watched Belle sit bolt upright on Philly with her shoulders raised. As he urged his horse to walk beside her, he caught a glimpse of Belle's deep frown. Even though she was troubled, he couldn't help but notice the way her lips pouted, and the sight awakened a deep primal hunger. The sudden urge to take Belle's face in his hands and graze her pretty lips with his thumb became all-consuming. He subconsciously licked his lips, as though his body knew exactly what his mind lingered on. But he set his jaw to repress his feelings.

The gray sky was clear, sending a cool, harsh breeze through the trees, ruffling the leaves, and the dark wispy hairs around Belle's face flew backward. Her long braid bobbed against her cloak just as Nathaniel thought about tracing the braided hair with his fingertips. When Belle's big brown eyes blinked in his direction, his heartbeat picked up.

"We're almost there," she said. Nathaniel pushed his nerves aside and gave her a firm nod, then looked ahead. As they passed a nearby tree, Nathaniel noticed the wooden sign nailed to the trunk. "Villeneuve," he read it aloud, then hummed in thought.

"My father used to tell me stories about our ancestors who crossed the shores and settled here," Belle said. "Remind me to take you to the bakery to try the bread. There's nothing more comforting than a crisp baguette fresh out of the oven." Belle's eyes glazed over, and her frown disappeared as she became lost in her memory.

"That's good," Nathaniel said as they left the forest and entered a bustling village. "Because I'm starving."

Wagon wheels squeaked as carriages bobbed along the cobbled streets, smoking chimneys flooded the sky with thick clouds, and the happy chatter of the women and children going about their day caught Nathaniel by surprise. He had been so consumed by stress, and seen so many horrors, he had forgotten that normal life still existed for people.

Market stalls lined the streets, and merchants shouted at the passersby, offering all manner of fine jewelry and clothing. A couple of men walked past, having an animated conversation in a foreign tongue. Nathaniel wondered what language they were speaking when Belle slowed her horse to a halt. Her face paled as she looked directly ahead. Nathaniel followed her line of sight to a stone fountain in the square, but then he noticed she wasn't staring at the fountain. She was gaping at the red sunset dipping in the horizon.

"Is everything all right?" he asked. Belle didn't say anything, but Nathaniel got the feeling that everything was not all right. Not at all.

Belle froze. Staring ahead with eyes unblinking, she clenched the reins so tightly, the whites of her knuckles were beginning to show. "I can't do this. I can't see my father tonight," she whispered.

Nathaniel opened his mouth to reassure her, but in a flash, she dismounted her horse and tied the reins to a wooden pole. Nathaniel followed suit. With the horses safely tied, Belle wiped her palms on her cotton pant legs. "How about a drink?" She pointed at the squeaky iron tavern sign swinging above their heads, and Nathaniel watched as two men burst out of the door, chuckling a little too loudly.

"You think that's a good idea?" he asked, unable to hide his disapproval. He knew Belle was anxious about being reunited with her estranged father after all these years, but the thought of the reunion taking place while she was tipsy didn't sit right with him. But Belle didn't stop to argue. She boldly marched through the door. Despite all of his senses telling him this was a bad idea, Nathaniel followed.

The air inside the tavern was heavy with smoke. It stuck to the back of Nathaniel's throat and didn't budge when he coughed into his fist. The floorboards creaked as they walked to the bar, and a sea of eyes followed Belle as she ordered the strongest drink on the wall.

"What's a nice lady like you coming in here drinking alone for?" the barmaid asked, dragging a tankard across the bar and pouring dark liquid into it. Before Belle could reply, Nathaniel sat beside her.

"She's not drinking alone," he said to the redhead behind the bar. "I'll have what she's having."

The barmaid's thin lips curved up for a flicker of a second before she busied herself making him a drink. "Suit yourself. I'll leave you two to wallow." The young woman walked over to the other side of the bar and picked up a rag.

The deep rumble of voices flooded the tavern, and judging by the disgruntled looks and slumped shoulders of the participants, Nathaniel knew this was the place people came to drown their sorrows. Unlike the other taverns he had been to, where travelers ate food and shared stories from the road, this one only served the local men and women.

Nathaniel wondered what the men of

Villeneuve had to mope about. The village had plenty of produce. None of their buildings had been burned down. Even the trees looked more lush and green.

Belle stared at the glass cradled in her hands and huffed. "I thought I could do this, but I can't."

Nathaniel took a swig of his drink, his face twisting at the tartness as he waited for her to continue. She pulled in a shuddering breath, then downed the rest of her drink.

"I don't think my father wants to see me."

Nathaniel eyed the worry lines between Belle's brows. "Why wouldn't he? He's your father, Belle. And by things you've said about him, he sounds like a wonderful man who would be ecstatic to see you."

"I left without so much as a goodbye," she confessed. "He probably thinks I'm dead. And what could I possibly say to justify disappearing without a trace?"

Nathaniel put an encouraging hand on her shoulder. "Tell him the truth."

She turned to meet Nathaniel's gentle eyes. "My father doesn't know what I am. What I became."

Nathaniel frowned. "Do you think he wouldn't approve?"

Belle shook her head, and he dropped his hand. "It's not that."

"Then what is it?" he asked, searching for her eyes.

"When I first turned into... you know," she said, staring into her drink. "I wasn't stable. I lost my humanity and was driven only by instinct. I was a monster and I ended up killing someone very dear to me."

Nathaniel looked shiftily across the tavern, uneasy at how loud Belle was talking. Though everyone looked too involved in their own conversations to be troubled by Belle's mutterings.

He leaned closer to Belle and lowered his voice. "Is that why you left?"

Belle nodded. "The thought of hurting my father..." She pressed her eyes shut. "I couldn't risk being around him. I didn't have control over... myself. And tonight, out of all nights, is a blood moon." She waved at the barmaid to fill her glass with another drink. "I can't be around him on a blood moon. It's too dangerous."

He waited until the barmaid walked away, then turned to Belle with a quizzical look. "What's so dangerous about a blood moon?"

"Every emotion becomes stronger," Belle explained. "Anger, confusion, love—"

"Passion?" He caught her eyes and held her gaze. His stare was intense, and he could tell she was barely breathing, but then she pulled her hand away and reached for her drink. He shook his head, trying to tame his thoughts. "This is about the beast, isn't it?"

Belle choked on her drink, then brought a hand to wipe her mouth. "Pardon me?"

"I overheard Will and Red talking," Nathaniel confessed. "He said he didn't like that you kept going after the beast by yourself. He went on and on about how dangerous and unstable he was, and how many people he'd killed. But Belle…" Nathaniel reached for Belle's hand and gave it a light squeeze. "You are nothing like that beast. So you lost control in the beginning and someone died, that doesn't make you a killer. It was an accident. But you're not unstable anymore. I mean, look at me…" He flashed her a smile. "I've been with you for some time now, and not once have you harmed me. On the contrary, you've saved my life."

Belle's eyes were gentle as she took in every word. "It's not that," she confessed, lowering her eyes.

The door opened with a bang, and Nathaniel picked up the heavy thudding of boots approaching him before he let go of Belle's hand and turned to see who had come in.

"Gunter, how nice to see you dropping by," the barmaid said, delighted. Her face beamed with color and glowed red like a flame as she hurriedly smoothed her hair and flashed him a glittering smile. "Shall I get you the usual, love?"

"All right, doll. You know what I like." The man wore hunting gear and had a string of rabbits slung over his broad shoulders. The shine of his black hair made Nathaniel wonder if the man used oil to tame his locks or if the grease was his own sweat.

The man stank of salt and dirt, but the barmaid seemed not to be bothered by it. On the contrary, she leaned over, passing him a tankard, and bit her lip, looking at him like a predator checking out its prey. The neckline of her cotton dress dipped low, giving the man—and everyone else in the tavern—an eyeful of her ample bosom.

"Looks like you got a few kills today, Gunter," the barmaid said, hovering around the man, watching him down his drink in several deep gulps. The tavern grew quiet when he slammed his empty tankard on the bar.

"These?" He gestured to the rabbits. Then he let out a hearty laugh. "These are bait, my lady. King Emmett is paying a handsome reward for every wolf killed, but there's only one beast I hunt now."

Nathaniel glanced at Belle. She sat still and stared at her glass just as before, but he knew she was listening.

"I've slaughtered three filthy mutts this week alone—"

Belle flinched and a hiss escaped her lips. Nathaniel shot her a warning look to stay quiet, but her reaction had already caught the hunter's attention.

"Well, well, well. What do we have here?"

He swaggered over to Belle, eyes glinting as they looked her up and down.

Nathaniel tensed, hardly breathing as he watched the man sit on the other side of Belle.

"It's not every day I see a fine specimen of a woman in this bar," he said, leaning into Belle. The barmaid huffed and straightened her dress as she glared at the hunter, but he paid no attention to the offense he had caused.

Nathaniel clenched his jaw, hating the way this man, Gunter, leered over Belle.

"What brings you to a dirty place like this, love?"

Belle remained deadly still, her eyes growing misty as she stared unblinkingly ahead.

"Cheer up, sweetheart. It's not all bad. Gunter is here to take care of you." Gunter grinned so wide, Nathaniel could see all of his yellowing teeth. Then he leaned in even closer and placed a hand on the small of Belle's back. "Why don't we get out of here and go somewhere quiet. I can take care of all your needs, then you can take care of mine?"

As soon as the words left his mouth,

Nathaniel stood up and tapped the man on the shoulder. "Leave her alone."

Gunter turned. "And you are?" he asked, looking at Nathaniel like he was a pile of manure.

"I won't tell you again," Nathaniel warned him, staring the man down. Gunter's face twisted into a scowl, and Nathaniel figured it must've been rare for anyone to stand up to him.

Gunter rose to his feet with a chuckle, but then pulled his arm back and swung his fist toward Nathaniel. He ducked, surprisingly quick, then punched the man so hard that the force sent Gunter in the air until he crashed with his back against a wooden table behind him. He then fell on the floor with a heavy thud.

Gunter groaned, and Belle jumped from her stool, watching Nathaniel with a mixture of admiration and disbelief.

"Ready to go?" Nathaniel asked, motioning toward the door.

She smiled, staring at him, still mesmerized by his newly found confidence. She started toward the door, but then stopped, turned on her heel, and kicked the man's shin. "That's for being a monster," she said acidly. Then they hurried out of the tavern, not looking back.

As they mounted the horses, Belle looked over at Nathaniel with her cheeks flushed. "Okay. I'm ready now."

A smile spread across Nathaniel's face. "Lead the way."

The sky grew black when they reached the house. Nathaniel tried to ignore his throbbing knuckles as he tied the horse and followed Belle up the garden path.

"Well, that's odd," Belle said thoughtfully. The soft moonlight barely lit up their way, and the house loomed over them. "Father always has his fire burning by nightfall."

As they reached the porch, Belle let out a sharp breath, and one of her hands found Nathaniel's. She squeezed it hard, and even though it was the same aching hand that punched Gunter, Nathaniel didn't mind.

"What's wrong?" he asked.

Belle leaned forward and pushed against the door. It slowly opened with a squeal that echoed inside, and a little gust of wind flew past them. Goosebumps rose on Nathaniel's forearms, and the hairs on the back of his neck stood on end as they stepped inside.

"Papa?" Belle called out as she let go of Nathaniel and searched the house. "Papa, are you in here?" She lit a lamp, flooding the small room with light. A small couch sat across from a barren fireplace, and a large portrait of a couple hung on the wall.

Belle went to check the rest of the house, and Nathaniel rubbed his chin as he looked around. A stack of notebooks lay on a shelf and a pile of iron screws and work tools littered the table. But most of the things were dusty, as if no one had been there for a while. "Are you sure he still lives here?"

Belle returned shortly after, shaking her head. "He's gone." But in her hands, she held a glass dome with a single red rose inside, standing upright.

"Is that…?"

"A wild red rose, yes." Belle placed it on top of the small wooden table by the sofa and stared at it. "It's a collector's item, very rare to find. It always grows alone and in the wild. I picked it with my dad when I was little, and judging by how most of its petals have fallen, I believe my father must've opened the glass dome."

"No matter. I can make the cure with what is left," Nathaniel said. "What about your father? Any idea where he could be?"

Belle looked around with a frown. "All I know for sure is that it's not like him to be gone at night." Her eyes flickered to meet Nathaniel's gaze for a moment before she turned away. "Maybe we can give it a day to see if he shows up?"

Nathaniel nodded. "I'll wash up and then help make some food."

After he finished his bath, Nathaniel went to the kitchen, lit the stove, and prepared a potato and onion stew. When Belle returned, her hair was neatly tied back, and she dangled a bottle in front of her with a grin.

"Look what I found," she said in a singsong voice.

Nathaniel inspected the bottle. "Red wine."

Belle bit her lip and squealed with excitement, but then she looked at the stew and hurried to it. "You need to put some seasoning in this," she said, reaching for some herbs. "Otherwise, it's going to be bland."

Nathaniel wondered what Belle was thinking. After all this time. All the searching. She was back in her father's home, and soon she'd be able to live an ordinary life again. Now that Nathaniel's memories were returning, there was no reason for them to stay together. Soon, he'd make the cure, and Belle wouldn't need him anymore.

Then what?

He supposed he would have to confront his brother. But that was a thought for another day.

They ate the stew in silence and later settled by the crackling fire. Nathaniel glanced at the pile of ingredients sitting on the table and wondered whether he should start right away. But sitting on the soft couch with Belle made him hesitate. She reached for his hand and studied his reddened knuckles.

"Does it hurt?" she asked.

Nathaniel shook his head, unable to lie

vocally, but winced as she pressed on the bruises.

"I still can't believe you punched that man," she said. There was no disapproval in the tone of her voice. Instead, she grinned evilly. "I keep replaying the moment over and over in my head."

Nathaniel smiled. But then he remembered why he punched the man, and his face fell. "You were right. He was a monster."

Belle looked into the fire, biting her lip. Nathaniel watched the reflection of the flames dancing across her glassy eyes.

"I'm sure he's fine," Nathaniel said, giving her shoulder a light nudge. She didn't have to say it. He could tell she was worried about her father. "If he doesn't come around, we'll find him." His heart lifted at the thought of not having to leave Belle, even after the cure was done. Looking for her father would allow them to have even more time together.

Belle flashed him a sad smile, keeping her eyes toward the fire. "I just found out he lost his job," she said, her voice soft above the crackling of the fire. "I wouldn't be surprised if he traveled to find work. He's always been very hardworking."

When Belle's eyes dropped to his knuckles again, he got the distinct feeling that something else was bothering her. "What else is on your mind?"

Belle brushed the tip of her fingers over his reddened skin. The touch was soft, almost sensual. "Do you ever wish you could just switch off your brain?" she asked.

Nathaniel gave her a wry smile. "You mean like having all your memories gone?"

Belle rolled her eyes with a light chuckle. Then her face grew serious again. "I wish I could forget about everything."

Nathaniel studied Belle's troubled face for a moment, then she turned to meet his gaze with a pleading look. "Nathaniel…" Her voice was light as a feather, and her sweet breath brushed his face.

"Yeah?"

"Will you help me forget…" she whispered with a tone of sensuality he'd never heard before. "Just for a night?"

Nathaniel's heart thumped in his chest. Her rosy lips were pouty and plump, and he wondered what they might feel like under his thumb. Or how soft they'd be on his lips. He reached up and slowly untied her braid and tangled his fingers in her hair. It was softer than cashmere as he took a fistful and pulled her closer.

Belle made a noise of surprise, but she didn't push back. "Only if you want to, that is," she said in a raspy voice, as if his actions winded her. They locked eyes, and Nathaniel peered into her soul.

"I want to," he said softly.

Belle closed her eyes. "Okay."

Nathaniel unfastened the ties of her shirt with one hand as he rubbed the back of her neck with the other. The insatiable hunger that no stew could ever satisfy grew tenfold as Nathaniel licked his lips and soaked up Belle's scent. He grazed his thumb along her jawline and brushed her hair away from her neck.

"Nathaniel—"

Belle rolled her head back and gave a shuddering breath as Nathaniel pressed his lips on her neck.

"Tell me to stop, and I will," he murmured in her ear before he gave it a light nibble on the lobe.

Belle gasped in the most delightful way, and the sound made his stomach do standing backflips. Nathaniel teased the edge of her shirt to fall, exposing her bare shoulder. He made a trail of light kisses down her neck and over her shoulder as he tugged on her hair. The resulting moan that escaped Belle's lips awakened a primal part of Nathaniel that he didn't even know existed.

He let go of her hair and pulled back to look at her. The light of the fire danced across her exposed neck and shoulder. The heat radiating from Belle, coupled with the fire, set Nathaniel's body ablaze. He decided if he didn't do something to cool down, he'd pass out.

Belle must've noticed because she reached for the hem of his cotton shirt and peeled it off in a swift motion. The cool air zapped his body in the most tantalizing way.

"Don't stop," she whispered, trailing the tips of her fingers across his chest. She planted a hand on his hard pectoral, and her eyes darkened as she slid her tongue across her bottom lip.

Nathaniel had never wanted anything as

much as he wanted her at that moment. He pulled her onto his lap and groaned with pleasure at the weight of her pressing against his hips. She fit so perfectly on his lap, and his fingers traced the back of her dress all the way up to her neck.

"I need to taste you," he said, brushing her lips with his thumb. They shivered under his touch, and Belle leaned in.

He clutched the back of her neck as her hot breath tickled his cheeks. Nathaniel looked deep into her eyes, searching for a sign of regret or uncertainty, but she rolled her hips and moaned in a way that evaporated any doubt that she wanted this kiss just as much as he did.

Without another thought, Nathaniel lurched forward and claimed her mouth. Belle's lips were smooth like butter and tasted as sweet as strawberry. He was certain that kissing her would give him a sugar rush.

He rolled her over and laid her on the couch as he sucked on her bottom lip. She squealed, then cradled his face in her hands, kissing him back with such a fierce passion, he was certain he had succeeded in wiping everything from her mind.

He kissed her cheeks, then down her neck and along her collarbone before he found her lips again. They kissed until the need for oxygen overwhelmed them both. Nathaniel finally pulled back, and the two of them stared at each other, panting.

Belle stared up at him brazenly with her hair splayed out on the couch around her and chest heaving. And Nathaniel realized there was no going back.

How could he let her go now? Could she ever want to be with a tortured prince with no future? But just as the thoughts came, the primal side of Nathaniel pushed them away, and he leaned in once more.

CHAPTER 11

Belle

When Nathaniel's lips explored her neck, Belle's eyes rolled back while her mind spun with desire. She had never been kissed by a man like that, let alone touched. But even her best fantasy didn't come close to this. To the constellation of shooting stars in her stomach. To the liberation of a million butterflies fluttering and tingling all over her body.

She grabbed fistfuls of his hair and pulled him closer. Urging for more. Begging to be claimed. Even though his chest was already hard pressed against hers, she needed him closer.

A hungry growl ripped from Nathaniel's throat as he abided to her will and pressed himself harder onto her. At feeling the heat of his tongue on her skin, Belle just about came undone. A passionate moan escaped her lips as she gave in to a sensuality entirely new to her.

When Nathaniel pulled back, she opened her eyes to meet his gaze. When their eyes locked, Belle gasped. His eyes glowed like two suns, fierce and golden.

She pushed him off of her and watched as his eyes returned to his normal deep blues.

"Belle, what's wrong?" Nathaniel asked, horror framing his face. "Did I do something—"

"No." Belle looked away and jumped to her feet. "I'm fine. Everything is fine."

"Clearly, everything is *not* fine," he said, keeping his voice soft. "I'm sorry if I crossed a line. I thought this is what you wanted—"

"I did!" She swung around to face him. "I mean, I do. I still do."

He smiled. "Then what's wrong?"

Guilt squeezed her heart. He had the right to know the truth. He was the beast that had been terrorizing the villages, and that was the reason behind his blackouts. But they were so close to making the cure. Once it was ready, she was going to tell him everything. Then they could both take the cure together and move on to the next chapter of their lives. He could take his rightful place as king, and she could... move on with her life. Find her father and mend things.

"I'm sorry." Nathaniel stood and walked over to her. Every thought in her mind screamed for her to move away. To fight against the burning desire that still lingered inside her. But he reached for her hand before she could convince her heart that welcoming his touch was a bad idea. "I'm sorry if things moved too fast. I don't know what came over me."

She did. His primal instincts were rising because of the blood moon. As were hers.

"I'm normally not like this." He let out a light chuckle then lowered his eyes to their laced fingers. "I'm actually quite the romantic. Flowers, jewels, dinner."

"It was a great dinner," Belle joked, lightening up the mood, trying to get her mind away from the wonderful sensation of his thumb brushing against the back of her hand. And how she wanted that same sensation all over her body.

"Belle..." Nathaniel's voice was soft, almost begging her to look at him. She did. "I'm scared too. I don't know what the future will hold, and I can't stand here and make promises I won't be able to keep."

"You don't have to—"

"Please, just let me say this," he begged. "Even though my memories are coming back, when I look ahead, all I see is a thick fog in my path. I have no idea what I'm going to do, but despite all those uncertainties, I see you. By my side." He pressed her hands to his chest. His heartbeat thumped wildly against her palms. "You are the only light in this darkness, Belle. And if all the suffering I endured brought me to you, then it was all worth it."

"Don't say that." Belle pulled away and turned her back to him. She couldn't bear to look at him any longer. The guilt was too much. "You only feel this way because you haven't yet remembered any women from your past. But as soon as you do—"

"It won't matter," he assured her. "If I haven't remembered any by now, I doubt my heart's been claimed by anyone else." He came from behind her and touched her shoulders, and all she could think about was how much she wanted his lips trailing up her neck again.

"No…" She moved away from him once more. "Nathaniel, you are the rightful king. You have a throne to take and a kingdom to lead." She swung around to face him but kept her distance. "That's your future."

He frowned. "What if I don't want that future? After all, my brother's been handling the throne just fine."

"Your brother is an idiot who's been making more enemies than allies," she said firmly. "He's taxing the people an outrageous amount because he's letting himself be influenced by Prince John."

When Nathaniel didn't respond, she held his gaze. "The people need a king like you."

Nathaniel chuckled as if it were a joke. "Look at me, Belle. I'm no king. I'm just a man handing over his heart to the most beautiful woman on earth."

As much as Belle loved hearing his declaration, encouraging him to stay would be selfish of her. The people were oppressed and needed a king like Nathaniel to free them from their burdens.

"Do you not feel the same way?" he asked, sensing the sudden silence between them. "Have I been reading this all wrong?"

Belle sighed, then took his hands in hers. "You haven't been reading it wrong," she said, looking into gentle eyes. There was a hint of relief in his smile. "But you have a duty to your kingdom, and I will not stand in the way."

"I don't want you in my way," he said, lifting his strong hands to cup her face. "I want you by my side."

Belle reached up to touch the back of his hand, which was still holding her face. "I'll tell you what…" She offered him a soft smile. "Why don't we focus on making the cure, then we can revisit this topic after the blood moon has passed?"

Nathaniel arched a brow. "So, you mean to tell me that everything that just happened... was because of the blood moon?"

"During a blood moon, certain urges become stronger," she explained, tugging at his wrists until he dropped his hands. "Which would explain what almost happened between us."

Nathaniel gave her a crooked smile. "I must say, the blood moon has become my new favorite season."

Belle laughed. "Blood moon isn't a season," she said, nudging his arm playfully. But then pointed a finger to his face. "And stop looking at me like that."

His eyes were gentle but hungry. "Why?"

"Because…" Her playful smile faded. "It does things to me, and my self-control is hanging by a thread."

Nathaniel let out a long breath. "Fair enough."

"Well…" Belle stepped back before he reached for her again. Before his touch made her forget about all sense. "Have a good night."

"Goodnight." He glanced toward the sofa. "And if you change your mind, I'll be right here."

She suppressed a smile. "Try to get some sleep," she said, walking toward her old bedroom, leaving Nathaniel on the couch. "Tomorrow, we have a lot of work to do."

#

The next morning, Belle woke up to the aroma of eggs and herbs. She freshened up, brushed her hair, then made her way to the kitchen.

The house was empty, and surprisingly, Nathaniel was nowhere in sight. Just when she was about to call out to him, she caught a note pinned under the candle holder on the small kitchen table.

Went to hunt some meat for lunch. Will be back soon.

The thought of Nathaniel hunting made her stomach churn with anxiety. What if he shifted while he was out? Or what if hunting itself triggered his repressed memories?

She dropped the note to the floor and hurried out the door. The breeze outside was cool and refreshing, but it did little to ease her anxiety. When she sniffed the air, she was looking to pick up one scent in particular. A whiff of spearmint blew through, and Belle ran toward the woods.

She considered shifting, but the thought of being naked when she finally found Nathaniel didn't seem like the best idea. Not after what almost happened between them the night before. Besides, there was no need to panic. His scent seemed close enough.

She caught the sound of light footsteps and rushing water less than a mile away, and a wave of relief washed over her. He was still in his human form. She headed in the direction of the sound, which was farther into the woods. The day was bright, and the sky was clear, but being under the trees of the forest was refreshing.

After a few minutes, Belle came to a clearing that led to a vast lake. A rocky cliff towered over the water, and a gush of steady water dashed to the bottom of the lake, forming a waterfall. Vapors covered the surface.

Nathaniel's scent was strong, but he was still nowhere in sight. Her heart began to race with concern. What if she had tracked someone else? Or worse. What if he was there but something terrible had happened to him?

Bubbles came up from the water, and Belle stopped breathing. Her heart squeezed with fear as she slowly made her way toward the edge. The dark blue water went still again, and for a few heartbeats nothing happened. Then a hand broke through the surface and grabbed onto her ankle. She let out a piercing scream as she fell and crashed into the freezing cold water with a mighty splash. Her body stiffened. She floated for a long moment, then a strong hand grabbed her arm and pulled her back up.

It wasn't until her head broke through the surface that she heard Nathaniel laughing.

"I'm sorry," he said through his laughter. "I couldn't help it."

She scowled at him. "You are in so much trouble!"

CHAPTER 11

She reached for him, and tried pinching his bare stomach, but he kept swimming away. "You just wait…" she said, shivering. "Till I get my hands on you."

Nathaniel's grin grew wider. "Now, am I being punished or rewarded?"

Belle grabbed onto a rock by the edge and waited for her heartbeat to slow. "Come closer and find out." She narrowed her eyes at him, her tone a lot more daring than inviting.

"So dramatic," he teased, still smiling. "It's only water."

She lunged toward him and pushed his head into the water. He swam to the bottom, bubbles of air tickling her legs as he laughed. Once he freed himself, he swam toward the plunging waterfall.

Belle followed after him until they crossed over the thick foaming sheet. She blinked the water from her eyes only to catch Nathaniel rising to a shallow rocky ground with the water up to his waist. Just beyond him was a cave, the walls reflecting the iridescent water.

The morning sun broke gently through the cracks in the wall, illuminating just enough for her to see the water drops glistening on

Nathaniel's skin, and sliding down his smooth back.

An amused smile grew on his lips as he glanced over his shoulder to make sure she was still following him.

Once Belle's feet found the ground, she stood. The water came up to her waist. Nathaniel reached out an inviting hand. She sucked in a breath before making her way toward him.

"So…" He turned around to face her. "What do you think?"

"When did you—"

"This morning," he said, taking her hand and pulling her farther into the cave. "I couldn't sleep, so I got up just before sunrise and started on the concoction for the cure in your father's shed. It takes a while for the chemicals to work together, so I had some time to kill. Hunting sounded like a good idea, but then I found this waterfall and swimming seemed a lot more appealing. And now, here we are."

Belle looked around in awe as the reflected morning light swayed over the rocky walls. "It's breathtaking."

"Yes, it is," he replied, but his eyes weren't on the cave. They were on her.

A wave of heat washed over her body as she turned to meet his gaze. Without another thought, Belle grabbed his face and pulled him down until his lips pressed against hers.

Nathaniel wrapped his arms around her narrow frame, but before he pulled her closer, she placed her hands on his chest and pulled back. Just enough to look into his eyes.

"This, in no way, means you're off the hook, mister."

He chuckled. "I wouldn't dream of it."

Then his lips were on hers again. She climbed onto him, wrapping her legs around his waist and weaving her fingers into his hair. His lips were soft and wet, and everything she'd ever dreamed of. Her body throbbed with desire. She moaned against his mouth, then parted her lips, urging for him to deepen the kiss. He abided, lowering himself in the water. She straddled his lap because she couldn't think of anything she wanted more. And when his strong hands slid up her thighs, her heart just about jumped out of her throat. She threw her head back, and he wasted no time exploring her neck.

But before things went any further, Nathaniel pulled back and waited for Belle to open her eyes and look at him. When she did, he let out a long breath and pressed his eyes shut.

"Are you all right?" she breathed, untangling her fingers from his hair and taking a better look at him. "What's wrong?"

"Nothing." He opened his eyes and offered her a breathless smile before reaching up to cup her face. "I just need you to know that…" He paused to take another breath, then rested his forehead to hers. "I'm yours, Belle. I'm yours, entirely."

"Oh, Nathaniel." She brushed his cheek with the tip of her fingers.

"Wait…" He gave a quizzical look. "Is this still the blood moon? Is there such a thing as a blood sun?"

Belle laughed. "No, there isn't," she said, still caressing his cheek with her thumb. "This is solely our hearts."

Nathaniel smiled. "Good, because my feelings for you are a lot stronger today than last night."

Belle leaned in and kissed him softly. "Mine too," she whispered. But as her fingers trailed down his arm, she felt something on his skin. She craned her neck and spotted a red rash on the back of his hand.

"What happened?" she asked, turning his arm toward the reflection of the light. Nathaniel followed her gaze but didn't seem concerned.

"Looks like some sort of allergic reaction."

"The sequoia essence…" Belle muttered under her breath, remembering what the merchant had said. "Wolves are highly allergic."

Nathaniel arched a brow. "I know. That's why I handled it without you around," he said innocently.

"Right." Belle shook off as much of the guilt as she could, then moved away from him. "Either way, we need to put something on it. I have cream back at the house."

Nathaniel touched her arm. "Why the sudden alarm?"

Belle forced a smile. "There's no alarm, it's

just that... my brother, Will, almost died from an allergic reaction once, and I just want to make sure you're okay." It wasn't a lie. He really did have an allergic reaction when he was little that made him very sick. But Belle never panicked. Not until now. "Can we *please* go put something on it?"

Nathaniel nodded. "If that'll make you feel better, sure."

She forced a smile. "Thank you."

They swam toward the edge of the rocks and climbed out of the water. "The cure should be ready by now," he said, picking up his outer garments from the ground.

"How many vials of the cure will you be making?" she asked, twisting the wet fabric of her clothes.

"There was only enough oil there for one dose."

Belle swung around, stunned. "What?"

"Relax..." He slipped on his shirt, then smoothed it down. "You don't need two doses. One is enough to do the job."

Belle's heart sank. She was counting on having enough for both of them. Of course she would never have forced him to take it if he didn't want to, but at least he would have the option. But now, it was either him or her.

"Belle, what's the matter with you?" Nathaniel touched her shoulder, snapping her back from her thoughts.

She stared at him for a long moment. *There was another way.*

While Nathaniel went straight to the shed, Belle ran into the house and grabbed her satchel. After flipping it upside down on the bed, a cloth fell out along with a book. Belle picked up the cloth and sat on the edge of the bed. She stared at it for a long moment, then unwrapped it until the glass casing with the dandelion came into view.

"No." She covered the glass with the cloth again and placed it at her side on the bed. "I shouldn't. Not at the cost of someone I love." There had to be another way. Perhaps, they could find more oil.

A sound came from the living room, and Belle looked up. "Nathaniel?" When there was no response, she stood and opened the door a crack, peeking out. "Papa?"

She caught a movement to her left, and she turned just as a barn owl flew in her direction. She ducked, covering her face. Belle opened her eyes just in time to catch the owl snatching the glass with the dandelion.

"No!" Belle grabbed the cloth from the claws of the owl and yanked it free. The glass crashed to the floor and shattered. The dandelion fell to the floor. The owl made a beeline across the room and flew back at full speed, swooping down with claws ready. Belle threw herself on top of the flower, and the impact knocked a pained breath from her lungs. The owl swooshed by, and she ducked her head.

The room fell silent, and Belle perked her ears. Once the wind beneath the owl's wings faded in the distance, Belle lifted her head and looked around. The animal was gone. Belle then moved her hand to examine the flower.

She gasped.

Belle had somehow blown the billowing tufts of the dandelion seedheads, clearing all the wispy seeds. She stared in horror at the disintegrated flower between her hands.

"No…" she breathed. "No, no, no." The merchant had warned her about touching it. About blowing onto it. She stared at her open palms for any indication that a wish had been granted.

What had she done?

The sound of glass shattering in the shed jolted Belle to her senses.

Nathaniel!

She jumped to her feet and ran to the shed. At barging through the door, Nathaniel swung around to face her.

"Belle, stand back!" he said, holding up his hands. The rash had covered both of his arms. "Take that vial on the edge of the table and get out. It's not safe for you in here."

"What's in the vial?" she asked, looking at the small blue liquid inside.

"The cure," he said. "Now take it and go."

Belle walked over to the table and pushed the vial back toward him. "You need to take the cure, Nathaniel."

"What?" He cocked his head, confused. "What would I need that for?"

Belle frowned, tears filling her eyes. "I

don't need it as much as you do. Now, please… take it."

Nathaniel's eyes began to glow a deep yellow. He turned slowly to see his reflection in a mirror. When he didn't flinch, Belle knew. His memories had returned.

He remembered *everything*.

CHAPTER 12

Nathaniel

"I have the stone, Your Grace," a submissive male voice drew Nathaniel's attention. He tossed his head from side to side, but everything was dark. A thick cloth covered his head, but the odor of iron and mold smelled like a dungeon.

"Good. Now, go and shut the door behind you."

Nathaniel recognized Prince John's voice. The squeal of hinges jarred Nathaniel's ears, and a door slammed shut. Nathaniel held his breath as he listened to the bolt lock.

"*It's just you and me now, Nathaniel.*"

Prince John dragged the bag from Nathaniel's head, and he blinked several times, focusing on the prince. His first reaction was to grab his throat and squeeze, but his hands were tied behind his back.

"*Tsk. Tsk. No need to look at me like that,*" Prince John said in a silky tone. His lips curled up as he stared at him with glinting eyes. "*You brought this upon yourself. I warned you what would happen if you didn't agree to an alliance.*"

"*I could never give you my sister,*" Nathaniel whispered vehemently.

Prince John shushed him by raising a finger. "*That's too bad. But you see, I've been having a chat with your brother, Emmett. And it turns out, he's much more reasonable. I daresay I think he will be a much better King.*"

Nathaniel eyed the chunk of iron in Prince John's hands. "*You can't lock me up forever,*" he said. "*You think your men will be quiet about this? Word will spread. And when my people find out what you've done…*"

"*That is precisely why I had this made,*" Prince John cut in, raising an iron mask in the air.

Nathaniel swallowed hard, unable to fathom how

Prince John could be so evil. He set the mask aside and picked up a needle.

"You won't get away with this."

"No one knows you're here," he whispered, sending a chill down Nathaniel's spine. The Prince lowered to meet his gaze, and Nathaniel set his jaw as two inky eyes bore into him.

"What is that?" Nathaniel asked, eyeing the needle.

"A different path," he added, waving the needle in front of him. He roughly grabbed his arm, then Nathaniel felt a pinch. A sudden burning sensation shot all the way to his heart, and a jolt sent his eyes rolling to the back of his head.

Every part of his body trembled and burned in an invisible fire. He jerked violently, ripping the back of his throat with an agonizing scream. Then he changed. His vision grew crystal clear, and he stood on four legs, arching his back and baring his teeth at the wicked prince with a snarl.

The Prince took out a necklace with a glowing iridescent stone. He raised a finger. "Ah, ah."

Nathaniel stopped, unable to move his limbs as he glowered at the grinning prince.

"Now, bow to me."

Without a moment's thought, Nathaniel found himself bowing.

The Prince cackled, placing the necklace over his neck. "Now you're mine, beast. And when I'm done with you, you'll wish I slaughtered you."

"Nathaniel! Please…" Belle's eyes came back into view as Nathaniel blinked, overwhelmed by the memory.

He *was* the beast. He fell to his knees, the weight of the memories pressing him to the ground. "I'm a monster. I've done terrible things," he said, his voice not sounding like his own.

Belle's eyes grew misty as she watched him with pleading eyes.

Everything was coming back to him at such mind-bending speed it crashed over him with a tsunami of grief.

The endless nights, howling in the night, gnashing his teeth, and attacking the villagers. He could even taste the memory of the metallic blood from his victims. So much blood. The innocent pleas. The wailing of loved ones witnessing the horrifying acts.

"*I'm* the beast," he confessed, his voice hollow.

Tears rolled down Belle's cheekbones. "It's all right," she said. But the look on her face told him it was not. And the only thing more painful than the memories was the fear in Belle's eyes as she looked at him while she hung upside down on a tree. Then again at his sister's home. He shifted right in front of her, and two women in his life whom he loved the most had stared at him with dread in their eyes. He turned away, shutting his eyes with a hiss. Then he realized… if Belle saw him shift then that meant…

"You knew?" He shot his eyes open and looked at her once more. Belle hugged herself, biting her lip, but Nathaniel's chest throbbed as his breathing quickened. "You knew, and you didn't tell me?"

All that time, she knew he was the beast. Knew what he had done. The thought was deplorable. "How could you hide this from me?"

Belle opened and closed her mouth several times, but no sound came out. Nathaniel tried to ignore the terrible itch growing up his arms and panted, his emotions swirling like a tornado inside his body threatening to tear him apart from within.

"I can't stay here," he said through gritted teeth, rising to a stand. His whole body burned and trembled. He could feel the change happening, but this time he was in control. Belle took a step back.

"Nathaniel, please. Take the cure. I am begging you."

Nathaniel turned away, unable to look her in the eye anymore. After everything he had done, he didn't deserve the cure. The only thing he deserved was a silver blade to the heart.

He stumbled out of the shed, and everything in his body shuddered. Then he shifted and took long, painful breaths. For the first time, he was entirely aware and in control. He stood tall and menacing, towering over Belle.

"Nathaniel, don't go," Belle whispered. But it sounded like a piercing scream in his ears. Nathaniel's heart flinched, but he shook his head to rid the sensation. He bounded forward and settled on his hind legs, then he stretched his back and howled. The release was liberating. The power pumping through his vein was unlike anything he'd ever experienced.

Then, without looking back, he charged forward, leaving the shed and disappearing into the forest.

CHAPTER 13

Belle

Belle sprinted through the forest in wolf form. Being able to shift was bittersweet for Belle. Part of her wanted the wolf gone, but another part of her couldn't be more thankful for the wolf's speed at that moment.

Another part entirely was terrified at what the dandelion seedhead had actually done to her, and what the consequences would come from it. But it wasn't the time to think about that. There was too much happening already, and she needed to get to Nathaniel before he did something he would later regret.

Nathaniel's image surfaced in her mind. The innocence in his eyes when she first met him. The loving man he'd become over the weeks with her, and the way he declared his love for her at the waterfall. So many different facets of him captivated her. But then he shifted, and his crimson eyes were so full of suffering and turmoil, her heart just about shattered on the spot.

Belle didn't know what his memories were like, but she imagined they were very dark. She could see it in his eyes. She hated that such a loving man like Nathaniel had to endure so much pain, and now she added to that pain with her betrayal. She knew what he was and didn't tell him, and at that moment, he didn't feel worthy of life. If anything happened to him, she would never forgive herself.

Belle sniffed the air. Nathaniel's scent was faint which meant he was a lot farther away than she thought, but he was headed north. There was only one reason he would head in that direction, and the thought sent chills down Belle's spine.

Emmett.

Belle pushed her legs harder. Her mind was solely focused on getting to Nathaniel. If Emmett really did sell his brother to claim the throne, then she wouldn't put it past him to kill Nathaniel with his silver sword. And an elven metal would certainly pierce Nathaniel's impenetrable skin.

But Nathaniel knew that.

Was that what he wanted? For his brother to end his misery? Was living with the guilt too much for him to bear? If that was the case, there was no way he would listen to her if she tried to stop him. He'd already been ignoring her. She'd been trying to reach out to him with her mind since he left, but he hadn't responded. He was hurt, and he had every right to be. But maybe, just maybe, there was still someone else that could reason with him.

---

*B*elle arrived in Sherwood Forest with her muscles aching. The people watched her with wide eyes as she made her way toward Marian's home, panting. They didn't seem nearly as shocked to see a wolf since Will had become the alpha. Though not everyone seemed comfortable, no one ran scared either. Will had done a great job at assuring the people that wolves needn't be feared. It filled Belle with pride at seeing what a great leader he'd turned out to be.

Belle closed her eyes and focused. Normally, she would have picked up his voice by that point, or Red's. Or even Marian. But Belle's mind was silent. When she opened her eyes, the ground began to move like a cruel vertigo spell. Nausea rose from the pit of her stomach as her mind continued to spin. She stopped and took a deep breath, but then fell to the ground with a thud. Something was seriously wrong. Her eyes rolled back as her mind echoed one last thought.

Will, help me.

Belle heard low murmurs before she even opened her eyes. She tried to sit up, but her body ached beyond anything she'd ever experienced. The nausea was gone, but a pounding headache had taken its place.

She looked around and recognized Marian's home. When she spotted Will and Red across the room, a wave of relief washed over her. He had heard her. He'd come to her aid, as he always did.

But they were whispering to each other something Belle couldn't hear. Why couldn't she hear them? Her keen sense of hearing would've picked up the sound loud and clear as if they had been talking directly to her.

"Will?" Belle called out in a raspy voice.

Will swung around, concern evident in his expression. He rushed to her side and helped her to sit up. "Belle, what happened?"

Belle rubbed her eyes. "I'm not entirely sure," she said, opening her eyes to find Red approaching with a glass of water. "How long have I been out?"

"Not long at all," Will said, taking the

water from Red and handing it to Belle. "Here. Maybe you're dehydrated."

Belle took the glass and downed the water in a couple of gulps. After she was done, she wiped her mouth with the back of her hand. "I need to find Marian."

Will took the glass from his sister's hand and placed it on the furniture beside the bed. Marian's bed. "She's outside with Robin. I don't know what she did, but he's not happy," Will said.

"Turns out The Snow Queen was the one who took him when he went missing," Red cut in.

"And that's not all she did," Will added. "She also froze his heart. If we thought he was stiff-necked before, you don't even want to see him now."

Belle shook off the nausea that was threatening to return. "I'm sorry, Will. It's not that I don't care, but I don't have time for this." She rose to her feet, ignoring the spinning inside her head.

"Belle, slow down!" Will grabbed her arms to steady her as she staggered toward the door.

Red moved out of the way. "Belle, talk to me. What's happening?"

"Marian!" Belle called out, holding onto the furniture as she stumbled toward the front door. "Marian!" Her friend appeared at the door.

"Belle?"

"We have to go." Belle moved away from Will and stumbled forward, grabbing onto Marian's cloak. "You have to come with me."

"Where?" Marian asked, alarmed.

"It's Nathaniel." Belle frowned. "He's going to confront Emmett, and I'm afraid of what will happen. You're the only one he might listen to."

"Why wouldn't he listen to you?"

Belle shook her head. "It's a long story, but if you don't come, Emmett just might kill Nathaniel. Please, Marian. Come with me."

"Okay." Marian nodded. "Let me get my satchel."

"Please, make haste," Belle pressed, walking outside. The sun had started to set, but the cool breeze helped with the vertigo and nausea. She sucked in a deep breath, knowing that even though she felt horribly sick, shifting was the only way she would make it to Emmett's castle in time. So, she closed her eyes and willed her mind to shift.

But nothing happened.

Belle opened her eyes, a wave of dread washing over her.

"What's the matter?" Will touched her shoulder, then studied her for a moment.

"The dandelion seedhead," Belle whispered, turning to meet her brother's eyes. "It worked."

"What worked?"

"I can't shift," she breathed. "The wolf is gone."

Will's brows shot up. "Isn't that what you wanted?"

"No. I mean, yes…" She shook her head, trying to get her thoughts in order. "But not right at this moment. I need the wolf right now. I need to get us to Emmett's castle as quickly as possible."

"I'll take you," he offered.

"You can't." She gave his arm a grateful squeeze. "It's too risky. Emmett has sent out a reward for every wolf to be killed. And the closer you get to his castle, the more traps have been set. The pack cannot lose their alpha."

Will turned toward the forest as if someone had spoken to him, but Belle didn't hear anything. Then, with a single authoritative nod from Will, Levi, one of the wolves from Will's pack, stepped out from behind a tree in his wolf form. "Levi is volunteering."

Belle's heart swelled with gratitude. Levi was the youngest of the wolves, but in her opinion, one of the most courageous. "Thank you," she whispered to Levi. He bowed his head in return. Belle then turned to her brother and pulled him into a tight hug. "I won't let him near the castle."

"I'm ready," Marian walked out, wrapping her satchel over her shoulder. "Wait, where's Robin?"

"He took off on his horse," Red said, rushing to stand next to Will. "And he's planning to kill the beast."

CHAPTER 14

Nathanel

Nathaniel didn't care about the wolf hunters teeming the woods. Part of him longed for a hunter to take him out of his misery. Thick gray clouds covered the sky, and the howling wind picked up as he raced on. Twigs snapped beneath his paws, and it was a marvel how easy it was to cross the forest. He ran over ten miles before he had to stop to take a breath. Any animal that crossed his path scurried away. Nathaniel was the alpha of the woods. Even a grizzly bear cowered and ran in the opposite direction when he roared at it.

The soft peaks of the castle—his former home—came into view, and a mixture of emotion rose to his chest. He crouched low, like a tiger hunting its prey. A guard stood alone on the corner. Nathaniel looked from left to right to check if the coast was clear. Then he pounced on the guard and tossed him like a rag doll. The guard grunted as he hit the wall, and Nathaniel shifted into human form, stealing the guard's uniform.

Before long, he propped the guard up, dressed only in his undergarments. He took the guard's helmet and placed it over his head. Oddly, the weight of the metal helmet was strangely normal for him. Like coming home after a long time away. Nathaniel wondered just how long he had been the man in the iron mask. Had it been days, weeks, or months? He didn't know.

He climbed the castle steps and slipped in through the servants' entrance. He sniffed, picking up his brother's scent. Now he was in tune with his senses. He could make out the low murmur of his brother's voice in the library.

He hurried down the hall, having no idea what he might say or do once he met his brother again. But every fiber of his being urged him on. He needed to see him, even if it was just one last time.

He burst into the library, and the door crashed against the stone wall. A cry of surprise followed, and Nathaniel rounded the corner and laid eyes on his twin brother standing beside a table.

"What is the meaning of this?" Emmett said as Nathaniel approached, disguised as a guard and drawing his sword. Emmett pulled out his silver sword in return, ignoring a shuffle of movement across the room, and looked at his brother again.

"What's wrong, not happy to see me?" Nathaniel asked.

Emmett's face paled, and he lowered his sword, staggering back.

Nathaniel yanked the helmet off his face, and Emmett grabbed onto the table, struggling to keep his balance.

"Brother?"

"How dare you call me that," Nathaniel roared, pointing his sword at Emmett. "After what you did to me." He pressed the blade up to Emmett's neck, but when tears welled up in his brother's eyes, it caught him by surprise.

"Nathaniel, I—I thought you were dead." The sincerity in Emmett's voice made Nathaniel pause, but he kept a firm grip on the hilt of his sword.

"You sold me to Prince John so you could take the throne," he said through a growl.

"No," Emmett said, his voice stronger now. He dropped his sword and raised his hands. "You were sick, so I made a deal with him. He had the best doctors and offered to heal you."

Nathaniel laughed darkly. "And you expect me to believe that?"

Emmett hissed at the accusation. "You were bitten by a wolf, Nathaniel. I didn't know what else to do. Prince John said he could keep you safe while they found a cure."

"I was never bitten by a wolf, Emmett," Nathaniel spoke through gritted teeth. "Prince John is the one who turned me into a wolf! He kept me in a filthy dungeon for five years, then found a way to control the beast in me."

Emmett blinked several times as his mouth dropped open. "What?"

"He used me to commit horrific crimes," Nathaniel went on. "Terrorizing the people and attacking the villages so he could raise the taxes and secure his position in the kingdom. He had me locked up in an iron mask to hide my identity so even his own men didn't know who I was."

Emmett's blue eyes pooled with tears as he listened. "Nathaniel, I had no…" His voice failed as he stared at his brother in disbelief. "Prince John told me you had died. He told me the treatments failed and that you didn't make it."

Nathaniel lifted his head to meet his brother's misty eyes. "And you just believed him? You didn't even ask to see me? Did you hate wolves that much that I wasn't even worthy of a royal funeral? Did I not even deserve that?"

Emmett made a noise of frustration. "I was presented with a dead wolf, Nathaniel. I was told it was you. I couldn't exactly present that killer to the people. Or bury it beside our parents."

Nathaniel clenched his jaw as flashes of memories crossed his mind of all the people he had killed. All the pain and suffering he had caused. He couldn't let that happen again. He sucked in a deep breath, then finally, he threw his sword aside and met Emmett's hard stare. "Then let's end this now. Right here. In human form. Then you can bury me beside our parents."

Emmett looked down at his silver sword sitting on the floor by his feet, and his brows knit together. For a moment, it looked like he considered the idea of killing Nathaniel, but then he scowled and met Nathaniel's determined stare.

"How dare you ask me to do that," Emmett hissed, his hands balling into fists.

Good, Nathaniel thought. He wanted his brother to be angry. His hot temper was the only way he was going to get him to do the unthinkable.

Nathaniel shut his eyes. "Don't think about it, Emmett. Just do it. You know you want to," he said, his heart racing so fast it sounded like a whole army marching in his ears. "You know what I am. You yourself said it, I'm a killer." He tried to keep his voice steady, but his arms began to tremble. The flood of memories continued to overwhelm his brain. Countless lives destroyed. So much suffering. And he caused all of it.

Then, he remembered the darkest secret of all...

Emmett threw a glass at the stone wall, and it shattered into hundreds of pieces. He was angry and yelling, his words becoming clearer as it surfaced from the back of Nathaniel's mind.

"You foolish man," he said, a vein popping from the side of his neck. "You know that wolf you were so determined to heal? It was the same wolf that attacked our parents."

He squared up to Nathaniel, anger radiating from his reddened face, but nothing could distract Nathaniel from the devastation in his eyes. "You are responsible! Their blood is on your hands!"

Nathaniel sank to his knees, the burden of his memories too great to bear. Emmett remained still, silently watching with a deep frown on his troubled face. "I'm the reason our parents were killed," Nathaniel muttered, the words cutting the back of his throat like daggers. He looked up at his brother with pleading eyes. "Emmett, please, end my misery. I don't deserve to live."

Emmett took a step forward and bent down to look directly into Nathaniel's eyes. Behind his hard look, Nathaniel saw something that made him feel even worse. Pity.

"After Mother and Father were killed, I made a solemn vow to hunt down every wolf in the forest. Then, you became one... imagine my horror. My own brother, who was going to be king, turned into a wolf."

Emmett looked away for a moment, shutting his eyes, and the weight of his words sat like an anvil on Nathaniel's aching chest. "I trusted Prince John. He promised me that he could cure you if we made an alliance, and if Marian married him. I did all of that for you."

"Then do *this* for me," Nathaniel begged, his throat constricting as he reached for Emmett's silver sword on the floor and handed it to his brother. "Don't let me live like this. I don't want to be a killer out of control anymore. Emmett, please. Just end my life."

Emmett retrieved the fallen sword before

he rose to his feet. Nathaniel panted and looked at the floor, waiting for his brother to strike. *Soon, all of the pain would be over*, he told himself. Soon, the world would be rid of a dangerous monster. No one would have to fear the beast anymore.

Nathaniel held his breath, listening to approaching footsteps and wishing Emmett would hurry. A rush of heat burned him from inside out as Emmett towered over him.

There was a moment of stillness, and Belle's face flooded Nathaniel's mind. For the first time since he got to the castle, he smiled. He wished that things were different. That he was a normal prince, and he met Belle at a ball. They would have danced the night away, Belle might have even laughed at his moves, stating that he must have had two left feet.

He wished things could be different, but that wasn't possible. Not when Prince John had means to control him. Making him a killer. He couldn't let anyone use him like a weapon ever again.

Finally, he opened his eyes just as Emmett raised his sword and directed it at Nathaniel's chest. "Strike true, brother," Nathaniel said, bracing himself.

But Emmett lowered his blade and shook his head. "No," he said, backing away and sheathing the sword. "I won't kill my brother." He turned and headed toward the door.

Nathaniel stood and followed him out to the courtyard. "Emmett," he said in a warning tone. "Do you not understand the implications?"

"I am not killing you, Nathaniel," Emmett repeated, crossing the courtyard as the gloomy skies loomed above. Nathaniel ran to keep up with his brother's pace then grabbed his arm and turned him around.

"You have to," Nathaniel urged, searching his brother's eyes.

Emmett refused to look at him, glaring at the floor instead. "I *can't.* I won't."

Nathaniel shoved him hard, then squared up to him like a wolf challenging the alpha. "You're the greatest wolf hunter in the kingdom. Well, now you've got a wolf in your castle. Slaughter it!"

Emmett's face twisted with repulsion at Nathaniel's words, but he made no attempt to draw his silver sword again. The gray skies loomed over them, and a chill in the air matched the feeling between the two brothers. Emmett crossed the cobbled courtyard and stopped in the center, looking up at the statue of the former King and Queen.

Seeing his parents' statue stirred up painful emotions in Nathaniel's chest, and he howled with fury and anguish. Every part of him hurt. Did Emmett not see it? He was drowning in his own guilt and shame. Killing him would have been the kind thing to do. Emmett never hesitated to slay a wolf before, so why the hesitation now? Then, struck by an idea, Nathaniel took a step forward, his expression serious.

"What are you doing?" Emmett asked.

Nathaniel bared his teeth and howled to the gloomy skies. Every part of his body trembled and burned in an invisible fire. He jerked violently, ripping the back of his throat with an agonizing scream. Then his vision grew crystal clear, and he stood on four legs, arching his back and baring his teeth at Emmett with a snarl.

When he caught his reflection on a

window to his left, he had shifted into the terrorizing beast with his crimson eyes glowing with fury. Emmett drew his sword at once and glared at the threatening beast in front of him.

"Emmett, no!" Marian's voice came from behind him, then she threw herself between her brothers with eyes full of tears. "Please, don't kill him!"

"Get away from him, Marian," Emmett demanded. "He's deranged."

"He's our brother!" she cried.

Emmett gripped his sword so hard his knuckles had turned white. Nathaniel growled, urging Emmett to do it.

But then an arrow whistled in the air, narrowly missing Nathaniel's ear and snapped in two against the statue. Nathaniel turned to find Robin Hood stepping out of the shadows. "The lady said stop. Oh, and look who I found." Robin pushed a man forward, revealing Prince John as he stumbled and fell to the ground. "He was trying to escape out back."

"You traitor!" Prince John glared at Robin. "I should've never hired you!"

Robin looked at the prince, unfazed. "I work for no one."

Prince John turned to look at Emmett with eyes wide with fear. "Emmett, this is all a misunderstanding. You have to believe me."

Emmett pointed his sword to Prince John, then motioned toward the beast standing in his courtyard. "You did this?"

Prince John's eyes shot up. "No! I would never! He was bitten by a wolf, remember?" He glanced at Nathaniel, who wondered why he hadn't pulled out the mermaid stone yet. Then he wondered if he didn't want Emmett to know that he had been controlling Nathaniel all this time.

"What I remember is you showing me a dead wolf and telling me it was my brother," Emmett hissed.

"I only did that to give you closure," Prince John replied, still on the floor, looking up at Emmett with frightened eyes. "The brother you once knew, the kind, loyal Prince Nathaniel, was long gone. His death was a mere formality. You yourself said it—your brother died the moment he turned into a wolf."

The words made Nathaniel's skin crawl, and he snarled. Marian shot Robin a look, and he stood cold and firm, staring only at Nathaniel with a bow aimed directly at his heart. Robin was protecting Marian, but Nathaniel would never dare hurt his sister. At least, not as long as he was in control of himself.

"Our alliance is over," Emmett snapped. But before Prince John could reply, the sound of scurrying footsteps caused all the men to whip around just in time to catch Belle entering the courtyard.

"Oh, thank goodness, you're alive," Belle whispered in a breathy voice as she stared at Nathaniel. But then her eyes locked on Prince John, and she scowled. "You!" Belle said in almost a growl as she lunged forward to attack the prince, but Marian grabbed her arms and yanked on them, forcing her to stay back. Nathaniel frowned, sensing there was something off about the way she looked.

"He's been controlling Nathaniel with a mermaid stone," Belle told Emmett, pointing at the cowardly prince who still had not risen to his feet. "Every single person your brother has ever killed was because he ordered it!"

A flicker of panic passed Prince John's eyes. He wasn't just afraid of Emmett. He was afraid of Belle, and Robin, but especially of Nathaniel. But as much as Nathaniel wanted to rip the prince limb by limb, he wouldn't do it in front of his sister. Or in front of Belle.

He turned to look at her. Seeing Belle again stirred up a fire from within. Suddenly, his anger toward her fizzled away as he understood why she kept the truth from him. She was trying to spare him the guilt. She was too good for him, and just looking at the devastation on her face was agony. He'd caused her enough pain, and he didn't want to make it worse.

"I did your kingdom a favor," Prince John said irritably, his face twisting into a wicked scowl. "If it wasn't for me, your people would have been ruled by a vicious dog."

Nathaniel took a menacing step forward, his nostrils flaring. Robin strode forward, his bow held steady.

"Robin, no. What are you doing?" Marian snapped, but her irritation couldn't cover the trace of panic laced in her voice. Robin's knitted brows twitched, and something flashed in his eyes. Though, Nathaniel couldn't understand what.

Emmett turned back to The Prince, who was still on his knees, and his expression grew dark. "Get up," he demanded, pointing his sword toward Prince John's neck as he rose to his feet. "Now, give me the stone that controls my brother."

Prince John gulped against Emmett's blade, then lifted his hands in the air. "I don't have it."

"He's lying!" Belle barked.

"I'm not!" Prince John glared at Belle, but then gave Emmett a serious look. "I swear on my life. If I still had it, I would have brought him back to the dungeon as soon as he escaped. But I don't have the stone anymore. It was stolen."

"By whom?" Emmett asked.

Prince John shook his head, but then gave Emmett an unfazed look. "Does it even matter?" he said, dropping his hands again. "You know that killing him is the right thing to do. Even *he* knows it."

CHAPTER 14

Emmett pushed the blade into Prince John's neck with a hiss. "You don't call the shots anymore. Now, answer me. Why did you do it? To charge higher taxes?"

Prince John gave Emmett a stern look. "This is about so much more than money, you fool. My brother is a weak man. The people of Sherwood love him, but they do not *respect* him. I've simply helped the people to understand that the world is dangerous, and they need protection. With that... comes a cost."

"You used my brother as a weapon," Emmett hissed.

Prince John pulled his fingers into a tight fist. "I will have the respect I deserve. And as my brother grows sicker, I will soon have the throne I was born to sit on."

"So you *are* poisoning King Richard! I knew it!" Belle yelled, struggling against Marian's clutches.

"Emmett, please..." Marian begged. "We're family. We must work this out."

Emmett didn't respond, but he met his sister's eyes for a split second. Prince John lunged forward and pushed Emmett aside, taking his silver sword and charging toward

Nathaniel with an ear-piercing shriek. Marian and Belle's rapid breathing told Nathaniel they were still there, but an eerie stillness fell on the courtyard. As if time ran slower.

Nathaniel did not want to be killed by Prince John. But if his brother refused, he wasn't going to put up a fight. He shut his eyes, silently apologizing to Belle in his mind.

A sudden shift in the air followed by a grunt had Nathaniel open his eyes again. Then, the courtyard exploded into chaos.

"No, you fool! What did you do?" Prince John shouted. The tip of the sword stuck into Robin's chest, who fell to his knees with a groan. He dropped his bow on the ground beside him, and Marian ran forward, screeching at the top of her lungs.

Before Nathaniel could process what had happened, Emmett roared like a lion, took two strides to Prince John, and after taking his sword back, he buried the blade into the prince's chest.

The death was instantaneous. He withdrew the blade from his flesh and pushed the prince to the ground. "I should have done that a long time ago," he muttered, wiping the bloody blade on his cloak.

"Robin. Robin, you stay with me, all right?" Marian said with urgency. She pulled Robin onto her lap while Belle ripped her cloak and handed the cotton material to Marian. Blood seeped from Robin's chest as his face paled in color, and his head rolled to the side. "No, Robin. You're not allowed to die, you hear me? I'm going to make you better, and you'll be okay." Marian took bundles of material and pressed on Robin's chest.

Nathaniel looked at his brother, who stood over the fallen prince with his chest heaving, and for a few moments, the king and the beast stood in silence.

"You were never the killer, Nathaniel," Emmett said, giving his brother a serious look. "He was. And now he got what he deserved."

Nathaniel bowed to his brother. He didn't need the throne, so any animosity between them was gone. But Emmett scowled.

"But that doesn't change how I feel about wolves," Emmett added, sheathing his sword.

"I can never accept you for what you are. I will renounce the throne, but I won't stay."

Before Nathaniel could argue, Emmett walked out of the courtyard and Belle dashed forward to call out to him. But before she could speak, Nathaniel's mind grew foggy, and his limbs moved of their own accord. His eyes locked with Belle's, but he couldn't make a sound. His mind began to darken, and someone else's voice entered his mind. Then, he darted across the courtyard.

"Nathaniel—wait!"

But he couldn't answer Belle's call. He turned and raced out of the palace grounds, obeying someone else's will.

CHAPTER 15

Belle

Belle firmed her grip on Levi's fur as he sped through the dark woods. She sniffed the air but didn't catch anything except the strong scent of pine. Her senses weren't as sharp anymore, and tracking would be nearly impossible, but Levi still had it. And since he was running without hesitation, she was sure he was on the right track.

Belle wondered where Nathaniel was headed. By his expression earlier, there was no doubt in her mind that he was being controlled again. And to make matters worse, he was headed to The Snow Queen's castle.

Belle should've known Aria was behind that. The thought should've crossed her mind the moment Belle saw the beast with the genie bracelet. Aria was the only one looking for the bracelet, and Belle wouldn't have put it past The Snow Queen to manipulate the beast for her own interests.

There were many things Aria had done, and as a forgiving friend, Belle had looked the other way, waiting for whatever phase that was to pass. But manipulating Nathaniel was stooping too low, and Belle was not going to stand for it.

By the time she crossed the bridge, she spotted the main gate hanging mangled on its hinge. No doubt Nathaniel had burst through without even slowing down. A wave of guards ran toward the castle, weapons at hand. Belle tried slowing Levi down, but he didn't listen. He must've been hearing them inside and decided Belle had no time to waste. He sped through the mangled gates then jumped over a group of guards, landing on a balcony above.

He stood on his hind legs, and after

kicking the door open, he sped down the hall. A piercing scream came from the ballroom, and Belle yanked at Levi's fur to go faster.

She wasn't sure what she expected to find when she burst through the door, but catching Nathaniel circling Aria like a shark in the middle of the ballroom was certainly not on her list of choices.

Belle jumped down from Levi then grabbed onto the railing. "What are you doing to him?" she called out.

Aria's eyes flickered to Belle. "Me? You can't be serious."

The black wolf snarled, and Aria let out a frustrated huff. Was he not being controlled anymore? Did he find out The Snow Queen had manipulated him and was now seeking revenge?

"Nathaniel," Belle called out. "You're not a killer. You don't want to do this."

Nathaniel kept circling Aria with the scowl of a killer, not even bothering to look up at Belle.

"Listen to her, you mutt." Aria glared at him, but still avoided making any sudden movements. "You don't want to mess with me."

Nathaniel growled as if daring her to fight back. Belle then noticed Aria was wearing the genie bracelet on her wrist. Now it made sense why Aria hadn't blasted him with ice. She was completely defenseless without her powers.

"Nathaniel, please…" Belle started down the stairs slowly. "I know you can hear me."

The black wolf with crimson eyes stopped circling, but still didn't turn to look at Belle. He kept his deadly stare on The Snow Queen.

"Listen to my voice." Belle lifted her hands in surrender as she approached. "You are the master of your own mind, Nathaniel. You can break free. I know you can."

His strong shoulders kept rising and falling as his breathing deepened.

"I know you're in there," Belle said softly.

Aria's eyes flickered to her friend again. "What do you mean *he's still in there?*"

"He's been controlled by a mermaid stone for too long," Belle muttered quickly. "You should know. You did this to him."

"I already told you, I don't have a

mermaid stone," Aria hissed. "And I hate those flipping mermaids. Control freaks."

Belle shook her head then stared at Aria with wide eyes. "Aria, who locked that bracelet on you?" Belle asked, keeping her voice low.

"Who do you think?"

The wolf snarled at Aria. She stiffened for a moment, but then glared at him. "What do you want from me, huh? Just say it!"

"Renounce your throne," a voice came from the top of the staircase. Belle swung around to find Snow, wearing a simple cotton dress and a maroon-red cloak. A snowy white barn owl flew overhead.

"Snow?" Belle's mouth dropped. "How did you…?"

Snow touched the necklace around her neck, brushing the iridescent stone with the tip of her fingers. "Roger took this from Prince John," she said. Though proud of the fact of having upped a prince, she wasn't smiling. She didn't seem happy to have resorted to such a strategy. But it didn't matter. Taking's someone's ability of choice and manipulating them was unacceptable. And no amount of remorse would ever earn Belle's forgiveness.

"Let him go," Belle hissed, balling her fists. "Or so help me heavens."

"I'm sorry, Belle." Snow kept her stare fixed on her sister. "Not until The Snow Queen renounces her throne."

"I will not," Aria said firmly. "Now stop this nonsense."

Snow lifted the mermaid stone and whispered into it. The wolf stepped forward with a low growl.

"Would you really kill your own sister?" Aria asked.

Belle couldn't tell for sure from where she stood, but Snow's eyes must have filled with tears because they glistened with the reflection of the chandelier. "You killed George."

"I didn't kill him," Aria said. "The lake is a portal. I just sent him to Jack's world—"

"You took him from me!" Snow cried. "I loved him, but that meant nothing to you. All you care about is yourself, and your high and mighty position. The people are suffering under your reign, and our parents would be ashamed of what you've done to their kingdom."

A flicker of sadness appeared in Aria's

eyes, but then it was gone, and she squared her shoulders, then looked up at her sister again. "If you only knew."

Before Snow said anything else, Levi jumped out from behind the railing and knocked Snow down on the steps. The necklace ripped from her neck, and the mermaid stone slipped from her hand, tumbling down to the main floor. Belle and Aria stared at each other for a few heartbeats, then jumped toward it. Aria snatched it from the floor then rose to her feet.

"Aria, give me the stone," Belle pleaded, still on the floor.

Aria stepped back with a frown. Then turned to the black wolf, lifting the stone to her lips.

"Aria, what are you doing?"

She whispered into the stone, then suddenly the black wolf turned toward Belle, his crimson eyes boring through her soul. Belle's eyes widened as he took a step toward her.

"No. Nathaniel, wait…" She crawled back as he approached. "This isn't you. You need to break free. Listen to me!" But he was already standing over her, and with an angry growl, he lowered himself and bared his teeth.

Belle sucked in a terrified breath, then reached up and touched his face. "It's okay," she whispered. "I know this isn't you. So, *please*, when you remember this, don't blame yourself. I'm not blaming you. You hear me? I love you, Nathaniel. I always will. For better or for worse."

The black wolf bared his teeth, his crimson eyes sharp and vicious, ready for the kill. Belle thought about closing her eyes, but she didn't. She wanted him to see that she wasn't afraid of him, and that she loved him... until the very end.

The wolf closed his eyes, and when he opened them again, the red had lost its glow. Belle watched as his deep blue took its place. Nathaniel shifted back to his human form, and Belle gasped as he fell to his knees in front of her.

She hastily removed her cloak and threw it over him, covering his waist. She cupped his face then lifted his eyes to meet hers. "I knew you were in there," she whispered. "I knew you were strong enough to break free."

"You freed me, my love," he whispered back. "You saved me."

He was looking at her like something had finally healed inside of him, like he'd woken up to find that his nightmares were just that, that they never existed, that it was all just a bad dream that felt far too real, but now he was awake, and he was safe, and everything was going to be okay.

Belle rested her forehead on his and closed her eyes, allowing her racing heart to slow. She couldn't care less that Aria had fallen to her knees with some sort of relief. Or that Snow was still trapped under Levi's massive paw on top of the stairs. All that mattered was that Nathaniel was finally out of harm's way, and never again would he have to worry about being controlled. Lexa had told them that if a man was ever to break free on his own from a mermaid's hypnosis, he was free forever.

"And I love you, too," he whispered ever so softly.

Belle opened her eyes but didn't respond for several heartbeats. Then she smiled and caressed his tired face. "I'm yours, always."

He leaned in and pressed his lips to hers. It

was soft but desperate, like he was running out of air, and somehow, she was his only source of oxygen. Belle reveled in his need for her, because she needed him just as much. He had claimed her heart, and despite all odds, there was no undoing it.

She was his... forever.

CHAPTER 16

Nathaniel

Nathaniel stood on the balcony to his room and looked up. The stars sparkled like diamonds in the night's sky above the castle. He inhaled deeply, taking in the pine trees and listening for anyone in distress.

But all he could pick up was the soft hoot of an owl, and Marian's light laugh at one of Robin's jokes.

A month had passed. Marian had been tending to Robin at the castle. The blade had damaged his nerves, rendering his left arm almost useless. But after a week, Marian was able to repair most of the damage. It also helped that his heart was frozen, so the blade never pierced it through. Robin being Robin joked that he didn't need his full range of motion. Even if he only had one arm, he'd still have a perfect aim and fight off anyone who might want to harm her. And he vowed to do just that for as long as she would let him.

Belle stayed at the palace while Nathaniel sent his guards out to search for her father, but their happy reunion never happened. No one in the village had seen him for weeks. Finally, a welcomed distraction came. Nathaniel's coronation. And having Belle by his side made his heart race.

Nathaniel drummed his fingers on the stone edge of the balcony and chewed the inside of his cheek. His royal uniform was tight and itchy. He tugged on his collar and swallowed. It would take some time to get used to wearing such restrictive clothing, but Nathaniel wanted to look the part.

"It is done. The decree has been made,

and tomorrow the grounds will be flooded with people waiting to see their new King."

Nathaniel turned at the sound of his brother's voice. "Are you sure about this?" he asked, looking at the bag on his brother's shoulder. "You don't have to renounce the throne. We can do this together."

Emmett refused to move from his spot by the door. "Will you be taking the cure?"

Nathaniel's brows shot up, but Emmett's demeanor remained unchanged. "Will you?"

Nathaniel frowned. "No."

Emmett pressed his lips tight and looked at the floor. "Then I'll be on my way."

"Why?" Nathaniel asked, moving Emmett to look up at him again.

"Nathaniel, I don't expect you to understand what I've been through while you were gone, but I do need you to know one thing. Just because I couldn't kill you doesn't mean I will accept you." The last words came out like a whisper but landed on Nathaniel's ears like a thunderstorm. He masked the hurt as he gave a nod.

"I understand."

Nathaniel had killed many people as a

beast. He knew it wasn't of his own doing, but none of the kingdoms in the Chanted Forest knew about Prince John's manipulation. They still considered the beast to have been the most dangerous creature in all the lands. If the truth was ever discovered, he was certain the vengeful attacks would come from all sides. He couldn't leave himself, or Belle, defenseless.

"Where will you go?" Nathaniel asked.

Emmett dropped his arms and rubbed the back of his neck. "I haven't decided yet. But rest assured, your secret will be safe with me."

The corners of Nathaniel's mouth tugged upward. "I'm sorry, Emmett... for everything."

Emmett half turned away and rested a hand on the door frame. "I'm sorry too, brother," he said through a heavy sigh, his shoulders sagging. "I wish things were different. Take care of our sister."

Nathaniel blinked against the burning in his eyes as Emmett walked out and disappeared from view.

But then a maid walked in and curtseyed. "Your Highness, the garden is ready for you."

Nathaniel's mood lightened as he smiled at

the young woman. "Excellent. Please have someone escort Belle to meet me outside."

"Of course, Your Majesty."

The royal staff had set up the garden with candles lining the path to the white fountain. A string quartet played whimsical music as Nathaniel strolled along the path. His heart sped up as he rounded a corner and squeezed at the sight of a young woman standing with her back to him.

He took a moment to take in the sight of her yellow gown. The material draped in waves with red roses pinned along the skirt. The tight bodice exaggerated her narrow waist and soft brown curls hung from the back of her head to the nape of her neck.

Nathaniel cleared his throat, and the woman turned, her dress swooshing. She was every part as beautiful as he remembered.

"Good evening, Belle," he said, grinning. She shushed him giddily, then waved him to come closer as she peered through a tall bush. "Is everything all right?"

"This is it!" Belle squealed as she grabbed Nathaniel's arm, pulling him behind the bush with her. Nathaniel followed her gaze through the leaves and spotted Marian positioning Robin in front of her.

"Will you please just stand still?" she grumbled. But he knew his sister. It was a flirty grumble.

"I'm standing like a statue," Robin replied, straightening his posture. "It's weird."

She crossed her arms and gave him a pointed look. "Do you want me to kiss you or not?"

Robin didn't respond, but he didn't have to. The way he was looking at her said it all. "I have so many memories of you, Marian. Even with this emptiness inside me, I still dreamt of you every night I was gone. My mind knows I belong to you, but my heart..."

Marian took his face in her hand, her brown eyes peering into his emerald greens. "I know," she whispered. "I hate that you were put through that."

Robin shrugged. "If it got me you, I would go through it all over again."

Nathaniel looked at Belle, her eyes glassy

with tears. "Shouldn't we give them some privacy?" he whispered.

Belle shushed him, then giggled again. "I want to hear this." Nathaniel didn't want to admit it, but he also wanted to see his sister finally find her happily ever after. She deserved it.

"I've been meaning to ask you..." Marian said, still holding his face. "Why did you do it?"

"Do what?" Robin asked, nonchalant.

"When you stepped in front of Nathaniel. You risked your life for him."

"I didn't do it for him," Robin said. "I did it for you."

Marian and Belle gasped in unison. "But your heart was frozen. I mean, it still is."

"But yours wasn't," he said, holding her gaze. "And losing him would've brought you pain. I didn't want that for you."

"Even with a frozen heart, you still care about me enough to—"

"Always." He attempted a smile, but before he said anything else, Marian grabbed his face in her small hands and pressed her lips to his. He stiffened for a moment, but then his arms wrapped around her waist, and he pulled her close.

Belle found Nathaniel's hand and squeezed, suppressing another squeal.

Marian pulled back and waited for Robin to open his eyes. "Did it work?" she asked, her voice soft but eager. When he didn't respond, her hands dropped to rest over his chest. "Please, say something."

Robin remained serious as he watched her in silence for several heartbeats. But then he gave her a lopsided smirk and swept her off her feet.

"That was not funny, Robin!" Marian slapped his arm, but that didn't stop him from spinning her around. By the time he lowered her to the ground, they were both laughing.

"Thank you," she said, looking up into his eyes. "For not giving up on me."

Robin held her face with both hands and looked at her deeply. The chemistry between them was tangible in the air. "Never." Then his lips were on hers again.

"I love you, Robin." Marian whimpered before kissing him back with such fierceness.

Belle squeezed Nathaniel's hand so hard, he thought for sure she was going to break it.

"I love you, Marian," Robin said, resting his forehead to hers, his voice a mixture of agony and ecstasy. "Now, come. I want to take you somewhere."

Robin took Marian by the hand and walked her toward a picnic laid out on the grounds. He picked up the picnic basket, and they walked away, arm in arm. Nathaniel and Belle exchanged looks, then Belle stifled a laugh with a gloved hand. Nathaniel didn't need to tell her the picnic was set up for her.

Belle and Nathaniel watched openmouthed as Robin walked a giggling Marian back to the castle.

"Unbelievable. He stole my..." But then Belle's velvety smooth lips found his, and all of his worries evaporated. She pressed her body up to his chest and his hands found her waist. When they broke apart, he suddenly remembered what he came here to do. "Now can I tell you how beautiful you look tonight?"

Belle blushed as she tucked a curl behind her ear, and Nathaniel was reminded of the night he first met her. She had worn her hair in the same way and had on a similar gown.

Nathaniel took a step forward, and Belle's eyes twinkled at him.

"What did you want me out here for?" she asked. Nathaniel clenched his jaw and glanced at the picnic that was supposed to have been for her. Now, the thought of taking Belle to the place Robin and Marian had kissed just moments earlier felt wrong.

Then an idea made him grin. "Never mind. I was planning to give you a gift later, but I think now is as good a time as any."

"Another gift? Wasn't this dress enough?" Belle asked through a laugh. Nathaniel took her hand and rested it in the crook of his arm as they walked back toward the castle.

"Has there been any word on my father?" Belle asked.

"Not yet, but my men have orders not to return until your father is found."

Belle bit her lip. "There's something I haven't told you," she said, lowering her eyes to the ground as they walked. "I accidentally used the dandelion seedhead to make a wish. The wolf inside me disappeared, but I still haven't seen any other consequence. I'm worried something might have happened to my father as a result of it."

Nathaniel stopped just short of the door and turned to Belle. He cradled her face with both hands. "We are going to find him. I promise."

Belle frowned. "Aren't you upset I'm no longer a wolf?"

Nathaniel smiled. "It's what you wanted, isn't it? Besides, you accepted me for who I am. It's only fair that I do the same."

Belle smiled. "Thank you."

"You're welcome. Now... your gift." Nathaniel smiled, thinking that there would never be enough gifts. She deserved the whole world, and more. "Close your eyes," he whispered, going to stand behind her. Belle's shoulders shook with a giggle. Nathaniel pushed open the door and guided Belle inside.

"All right, now open them."

Belle opened her eyes and gasped at the ceiling-high bookcases that filled the entire hall. Nathaniel had arranged for every bookseller in the kingdom to fill the shelves with the finest books that were ever written. Belle lightly brushed her fingertips along the spines of one of the cases and squealed. "There must be thousands of books in here," she said.

"It's all yours, if you want it," Nathaniel said, keeping his hands clasped in front of him. Belle stopped and looked at him with wide eyes.

He strode to her and lowered to one knee. "You rescued me from a monster. Then you helped me even when you found out what I was and all I had done," Nathaniel took Belle's hand. "I love you, Belle, and if you'll have me, I want to spend the rest of my life with you beside me. As my queen."

Belle rolled her lips inward with a smile, and her eyes turned glassy. "Just promise me something," she whispered. "Never, *ever*, ask Emmett to kill you again."

Nathaniel bowed his head, ashamed of the memory. "If you can accept me as I am, then I promise." He lifted his head just as Belle crouched and captured him with a kiss.

"Being your bride would be a dream come true." But then her smile faded, and she looked away. "I'll be darn…"

Nathaniel rose to his feet and touched her

cheek. "What is wrong, my love?" he asked softly.

Belle looked back at him again, a sparkle in her eyes as if she was seeing something for the very first time. "The book was right."

"What book?"

Belle wrapped her arms around his neck and flashed a smile so beautiful, he could stare at it forever. "The beauty really did... fall in love with the beast."

EPILOGUE

Snow White

Snow White hugged her knees and counted back from one hundred with her eyes closed. She hated dark and closed spaces. She gritted her teeth, trying to ignore the emotions raging in her chest. Her sister, Aria, had turned into a cold-hearted monster, also known as The Snow Queen. But Snow never imagined Aria would throw her own sister in the dungeon.

Perhaps Aria didn't expect Snow to turn

on her, either. But one thing was clear; the two sisters had changed.

The image of George being thrown into the lake burned in her memory and played on a loop whenever she was in the dark. She took a deep, shaking breath and listened to the steady drip echoing in the cell. Snow had no conceivable idea of what wretched plans The Snow Queen had for her now. She was capable of murder, and that knowledge was enough to make up her mind that she wasn't going to be a sitting duck and wait for her evil sister to return.

The welcome flap of wings lit up Snow's dark mood, and she opened her eyes, blinking in the dim cell just as Roger, her white barn owl, swooped in. A brass key dropped in her hands as he flew over her head, and he settled on the damp floor beside her.

"You are so clever. Thank you, Roger," Snow said, smoothing his back feathers with her index finger.

Aria has left the castle. Now is your chance. But avoid the main road. There is a royal engagement ball in the White Rose Kingdom, Roger said, his voice entering Snow's mind. She tilted her head as she studied the owl for a moment, wondering if she misheard him.

"Who's getting married?" she asked him. The owl shook his feathers like a wet dog and gave a hoot.

The new king is to marry Belle.

Snow's stomach knotted at the mention of the new king. Memories of what she'd done flooded her mind and struck her conscience. Nathaniel could've very well have put her to death, but he showed mercy. As did Belle.

Snow supposed that Belle might never forgive her for what she'd done. As much as it pained Snow to have lost a good friend, she couldn't blame Belle. It was wrong, and Snow knew it. But Aria needed to be stopped.

Ever since Jack left, she'd been cold and distant. And what she did to George was just the beginning of her evil course. Soon, she made an alliance with Prince John, who was wicked beyond belief. And she took to meddling in other people's affairs. It was like a game of chess to her. People were nothing but pawns, and Snow couldn't just sit back and watch.

She did what she could, but her plan

failed, and now she was locked in a dungeon. Though, not for long. Snow looked at the brass key in her hand. Escaping wasn't the problem. Now, finding another way to dethrone her sister, however, *that* was the real challenge.

She had to take another angle. And she couldn't do it alone. The Snow Queen was too powerful. Snow needed to make allies—strong and powerful allies—which meant... she needed to find a way to get Belle and Nathaniel back on her side.

She needed to apologize.

Determined, Snow took the brass key and stood. She brushed off her damp skirts and rammed the key into the lock.

There are two guards outside the door. I'll distract them and you'll have a clear path to the stables, Roger said as he took flight.

Snow threw the hood of her cloak over her head and carefully opened the metal door. She watched her barn owl fly up the steps and out the door and listened for a shout, followed by a crash.

She smiled. "Good boy, Roger."

She hurried out the door, then scaled the

steps, taking two at a time. As she reached the stable, she wasted no time untying Penny, her horse. "Hi there, girl. Are you feeling up for a ride to the White Rose Kingdom?" Snow said, smoothing Penny's mane.

I can't remember the last time we went on a trip, Penny replied with a neigh. Snow fastened the saddle and climbed on.

"Come on, then. Time for an adventure," she whispered in Penny's ear. It flicked back, and the horse galloped down the path and into the woods.

A symphony of music flooded the air as Snow and Penny reached the castle. The windows glowed yellow in the night, and a babble of excitable talk greeted them. Guards stood by the front gates, inspecting the line of carriages waiting to enter. Snow set her jaw. There was no way her name would be on the guest list.

She scanned the skies for Roger, but he was nowhere to be seen.

"Stay here," Snow whispered to Penny,

not bothering to tether her. She climbed up a tree next to the castle walls and peered over the top. A flood of regal guests filled the castle grounds, and all manner of fine wines and food sat laden on large banquet tables. Snow squinted and could just make out Belle standing near the center with Nathaniel. They both looked so... formal. It was a far cry from the last time she saw them, when they had both looked disheveled and desperate.

Finally, she spotted Roger flying over the band. She hooted to get his attention, and he changed his direction, landing on her outstretched hand.

Belle is in great distress. Her father is still missing. Nathaniel has had his men searching, Roger said. *Even her brother and his pack haven't been able to track him down.*

Snow frowned. "Crumbs. What do you know about her father?"

He's known to be the greatest inventor in all the land, and a collector of rare herbs and artifacts.

"Where do you think a man like that would go?"

I did hear a rumor from the other birds. But I'm

not sure how much truth is in it, Roger offered, ruffling his feathers.

Snow nodded. "Tell me."

Roger twisted his head around and gripped her wrist with his claws. *There's an inventor who has been selling his gadgets on the road. He never stays in the same place for longer than a day. But they saw him yesterday entering Quail Village.*

"That's less than an hour's ride from here," Snow said. A bubble of hope rose to her chest, and she dropped down from the tree.

She mounted Penny, then raced through the forest with Roger flying above their heads.

The village was unusually quiet, and the full moon lit up the streets in a silver glow. Snow kept her hood on and jumped down from Penny.

Belle's father should be here, somewhere. Roger's voice entered Snow's mind, but she wasn't entirely sure where he'd landed.

"Go and have a drink," she whispered to Penny, motioning to the water trough outside a tavern. Snow thought about going inside for a drink and maybe some food, but it was dark, and she was afraid someone would recognize her. Not so much as the Princess of the Chanted Kingdom, but as The Snow Queen's sister. She would surely be in trouble.

Instead, she walked the streets, scanning the crooked houses with smoking chimneys, wondering what it would be like to live a common life. A life without having to hide in a wine cellar. Or be imprisoned in a dungeon. Was it too much to ask for?

Though even before Aria killed George, and The Evil Queen murdered her parents, Snow's life was far from normal. If it weren't for her gift in talking to animals, she wouldn't have been able to survive all the loneliness.

She shook her head, determined not to cry. She was going to find Belle's father and finally reunite him with his daughter, and hopefully, gain her support in overthrowing The Snow Queen. Then she would finally get justice for her beloved George.

A grunt and a thud alerted her to a dark alley. Without hesitation, she ran to the edge of a building and peeked around the corner into the darkness.

A shadowy figure stood near a wagon of hay. When it turned around, the moonlight lit up a pair of brown eyes. Snow released a breath, then stretched her neck to get a better look. The man was older with gray hair. She had never met Belle's father before, but the resemblance was unmistakable.

The thrill of finding him before anyone else made her heart skip a beat. She took a step closer, but then halted when the moonlight illuminated a glistening bloody knife in his hand. Snow looked down to see a man dead on the ground, a growing puddle of blood staining the floor.

"I am done being the good one," the killer muttered under his breath.

Snow's heart raced. "Are you… Belle's father?" she asked, her voice shaking as the iron smell of blood filled the ally.

"Not anymore," the man replied, a wicked smile tugging at his lips as he raised the bloody dagger in the air. "Now I am Rumpelstiltskin."

--Find out what happens next in book 4 of the Fairytales Reimagined series; *Pure as Snow*. Read Now.

Join the Fairytales Reimagined community on Facebook to keep up to date on all the news, catch behind the pages action and share fan theories on upcoming books!

Made in United States
Troutdale, OR
10/16/2023

13753467R00181